E. R. (Edward Reynolds) Roe

Brought to bay

E. R. (Edward Reynolds) Roe

Brought to bay

ISBN/EAN: 9783337140861

Printed in Europe, USA, Canada, Australia, Japan

Cover: Foto ©Andreas Hilbeck / pixelio.de

More available books at **www.hansebooks.com**

BROUGHT TO BAY.

By E. R. ROE.

"Hard upon the hickory oar !
She moves too slow;
Time we were at Shawneetown,
Long time ago."

BOSTON:
ESTES AND LAURIAT,
299–305 WASHINGTON STREET.
1882.

CONTENTS.

CHAPTER.   PAGE.

   I. Adown the Wabash   7

  II. Cave-in-Rock   19

 III. Earthquakes   34

 IV. The Tippecanoe. — A Child's Religion. —
       The Cave.   39

   V. Government at the Circumference. —
       Divided Counsels   56

 VI. A Perplexed Frenchman. — A Rescue. —
       Backwoods Surgery   67

 VII. The Wounded Man's Story . . .   84

VIII. An Amphibious Town. — Worship in the
       Woods. — "The Jerks" . . .   92

 IX. Serving God on Trust 109

   X. "All the Pigeons in the World." — After
       the Wilderness, what? . . . 135

 XI. Doubtful Tidings — Hypochondria. — Sin-
       clair at St. Genevieve . . . 151

 XII. Three Years Later. — The Clew recov-
       ered. — Leyba in the Toils . . 168

XIII. An Interview. — Light Breaking in . 174

XIV. Virginia in Court. — Freeman Again. —
       Leyba 182

CHAPTER.		PAGE.
XV.	SANTA CLARA. — ANTOINE DE ULLOA	209
XVI.	FATHER AND SON	228
XVII.	A RIVER VOYAGE	237
XVIII.	IN THE SHADOW	257
XIX.	OLD TABBY'S STORY. — HO! FOR CUBA	263
XX.	A CATASTROPHE. — CONCLUSION	274

BROUGHT TO BAY.

CHAPTER I.

ADOWN THE WABASH.

A MORE excellent craft than the good keel-boat Tippecanoe never floated Indian corn to New Orleans. At any rate, this was the opinion of her commander, Captain Tom Summers. He stood upon the banks of the Wabash at Port St. Vincent, or Vincennes, as the Indiana town was more frequently called, and contemplated his vessel, ready laden for a voyage down the Ohio and the Mississippi, with as much pride as any old salt could feel who walked the deck of a full-rigged ship. His crew were all on board, and as he was about to push out into the stream, a gentleman came down the bank toward the boat, and, with a well-bred air, inquired if he had the pleasure to address Captain Summers.

"My name is Summers," replied the captain, with an inquiring look at the stranger. "What might your name be?"

"My name is Leyba," replied the stranger, "and

I come to request a passage on your boat as far as Shawneetown."

"Whar 's your traps, stranger?" said Tom. "We are just pushing her off."

"My baggage is at Shawneetown," said the gentleman; "I also am ready to move."

"Well, walk aboard, and we 'll soon bid Vincennes good by."

Without another word, the new-comer did as he was bidden, and quietly seated himself near the stern of the boat. The line was cast off, the bow of the boat thrown out into the stream, and the Tippecanoe was soon floating rapidly down the Wabash.

The sun had gone down, and it was already nearly dark; the river was in fine boating condition, and as his symmetrical craft glided rapidly down the stream, Summers held the helm, and almost instinctively controlled her movement, while he cast occasional scrutinizing glances toward his passenger. Finding him indisposed to talk, Summers determined to ply him with a few civil questions.

"You said your name was — ?"

"Leyba," replied the other.

"Spanish, is n't it?"

"Yes, Captain Summers; my father was Spanish."

The deferential way in which he pronounced

the words "Captain Summers" impressed Tom favorably. It indicated that he appreciated the importance of sailing with so reputable a commander. Still there certainly was a sinister look about the dark-haired stranger, and so, by mere association of ideas, without any suspicion as to the stranger's character, he added :

"They say them Cave-in-Rock fellers is Spaniards."

This was really intended as an interrogation, but Mr. Leyba (as he had called himself) either did not so understand it, or he purposely evaded it; he said only, —

"This is a fine craft of yours, Captain Summers. I think I know a good keel."

"I think the Tippecanoe is a right smart boat," said Tom. "Here, George," continued he, to one of the crew, "take the helm while the stranger and I turn in. Keep her well in the channel; it would be bad luck to run into the brush in this high water." Then, turning to Mr. Leyba, "Come below, and let me show you our inside."

As they turned to go down, the captain heard the sound of paddles; he stopped and awaited their nearer approach, and soon discovered a single Indian coming alongside in a small canoe. Without any ceremony, the savage climbed on board, hold-

ing a line from his canoe in one hand and a ham
of fresh venison in the other.   Recognizing Summers as being in command, the Indian held the
venison toward him, and in a guttural tone uttered
the English word he knew best : —

"Whiskee?"

"Yes," said the captain; "where's your bottle?"

The Indian laid down the venison, put his hand
into the bosom of his old buckskin hunting-shirt,
and drawing forth a long-necked gourd, handed it
to Summers.   Then, Tom beckoning Leyba to follow, both descended into the boat.

The cargo of the Tippecanoe consisted of corn
and whiskey.   But the boat was by no means fully
loaded, which Leyba manifestly observing, Tom
explained by saying that he intended to fill up
with salt at Shawneetown.   Summers then knocked
the bung out of a whiskey barrel, filled the Indian's
gourd with water, and, reversing it suddenly, thrust
the long neck into the whiskey barrel.   At the same
time he looked up at Leyba, and remarked with a
twinkle in his eye, "Turning water into whiskey!"

A few minutes sufficed for the water and whiskey
to interchange places ; and suddenly withdrawing
the gourd, and putting in a corn-cob stopper, he
carried it up to the Indian.   The savage took a few
swallows from it, and shaking his head exclaimed,

with well-marked disgust but in very bad English, "Too muchee Wabash. Ugh !" meaning, of course, that the whiskey had been watered. Then suddenly dropping over the side into his canoe, he soon disappeared in the darkness.

After partaking of the venison, and such fare as the boat's supplies afforded, Leyba declined to lie down, and accompanied the captain again upon deck ; and there he insisted on remaining until morning. Summers soon gave up the effort to draw his passenger into conversation, and devoted his whole attention to his floating craft, but some time about midnight, while he was trying to determine the position of his boat by uttering short, sharp whoops, and listening to the echo which came back, the stranger, as if forgetting himself, said, —

"She wants to go to larboard, Captain Summers."

Tom moved his helm accordingly, and remarked, in a tone indicating a desire for conversation, —

"You have got a good ear, Mr. Leyba. This is not the first time you have run the rivers?"

"Not the first," replied Leyba.

"You have been to Orleans, mayhap?"

"I know every bend from here to the Gulf"

Summers remained silent for a few minutes ; but the stranger's knowledge of the river won his admiration, and, taking a flask of whiskey from his pocket and offering it to Leyba, he said, —

" Take something, stranger ! "

" I thank you, Captain ; but I never drink anything."

A man who knew every bend in the Mississippi, and who yet never drank whiskey, was something too deep for the comprehension of Tom Summers ; and giving up all further attempts at familiarity, he called another man to the helm and turned in below for a short sleep.

The monotonous voyage upon the Wabash to its mouth, was continued without any incident of note, until the Tippecanoe entered the Ohio, and was moored at Shawnectown, about sundown on the next evening. Leyba thanked Captain Summers for the accommodation which had been extended to him, bade him adieu, and so soon as the boat touched shore, walked away and disappeared. After he was gone, one of the boat hands handed to Captain Summers a leaf seemingly from an old memorandum-book, which had been dropped on the deck by Leyba. On it were these words, apparently written some years before :

> " Angela with the black woman."
> " Known only as Virginia."
> " Limestone to Shawneetown."

Hoping again to meet Leyba, he put the paper in his pocket for safety, with no suspicion of any special interest attached to it. But Leyba was not seen again, and his disappearance remained, for the time, a mystery.

As Captain "Tom" Summers (as he was called by his friends and he appeared to have no enemies), played a principal part in the events of this veritable story, it will not be amiss to have a closer view of him. He was a characteristic and superior specimen of a now extinct order of river-men, — the keel-boatmen. Robust, muscular, hardy; generous, brave, intelligent in his proper sphere; master of river-craft, and a natural leader among the men of his class, — Tom Summers was a man showing in marked degree the effects of that broad freedom which is born of the Great West. He thought for himself, untrammelled by conventionalism ; and he added to much natural shrewdness a practical knowledge of men, acquired in his fifteen years of keel-boat life on the Western rivers. While, therefore, he was illiterate, — being barely able to read and to write, — he was intelligent as to matters not beyond his field of vision ; and as a brave and generous man, master of his vocation, he well deserved his eminence among men of his class. Such was the captain of the Tippecanoe.

As the ancient village of Shawneetown — ancient to the Indian tribes who formerly inhabited the place, — was the residence of some of the principal characters in our story, they will here be briefly introduced to the reader.

"Old Dan Rose," as he was usually called, had brought his family to this then rising village about two years before. The family consisted of himself; his wife; his grown son, Tim; his daughter, Mrs. Freeman; and her daughter, Virginia, who was yet a child. Besids these was an old slave named Tabby, who came with the family from Limestone (now Marysville) in Kentucky.

Mrs. Freeman — or "Katy," as her parents called her — had been married at Marysville. Her husband had treated her with such cruelty that she had been compelled to seek relief in divorce. But after their legal separation her late husband, Freeman, had kept her in constant terror for some years, by stealing away their child, Virginia, who had several times been reclaimed by the mother with great difficulty. A desire to get beyond the reach of her tormentor had induced Dan Rose, her father, to move five hundred miles down the river to Shawneetown. The mother insisted on calling her child by the family name, unwilling she should ever bear that of her father; and so the young girl was known in the village as Virginia Rose.

Two or three days before the arrival of the Tippecanoe at Shawneetown, Freeman, the girl's father, had made his appearance in the town. He had come down the Ohio in a small *pirogue*, with a load of flour and a small crew of his own negroes. After disposing of his flour, Freeman notified old Dan Rose that he came armed with the proper legal authority to reclaim his child, and that he meant to take her away. He soon found, however, that there was a higher law in the village than that administered by any of the courts. The citizens held a meeting, and notified Freeman that he would not be permitted even to see his child, much less to take her away. This decision was accompanied by such manifestations of indignant feeling as to convince Freeman that his effort was altogether hopeless. He then begged permission to see the child in the presence of her friends. This was granted him, and, hardhearted as all thought him, he wept upon taking his leave of her. This was only a few hours before the landing of Captain Summers' keel-boat; and the next morning at break of day Freeman started up the river on his return.

Within an hour after the departure of Freeman's

boat, the mother awoke, and found that the daughter, who always slept by her side, was gone. Alarmed, she hastened to her father's bedside, exclaiming with a cry of agony, "Tom Freeman has stolen away my child!" Without a word of reply old Dan Rose sprang out of bed, and within a few minutes the whole household were up. The neighbors were visited, but there were no tidings of the missing child. It was soon found that Freeman had left, and his boat was still visible some miles above the town, over the long reach of open water.

It was but the work of a few minutes for Tim Rose to gather a few trusty companions, who, with ready rifles and fleet horses, were soon taking the shortest route through the woods to the mouth of the Wabash ten miles above.

They reached the Wabash, entered a skiff kept there for ferry purposes, and gained the middle of the Ohio River in time to intercept Freeman. They entered his boat, told him their errand, and were permitted with apparent readiness to look for the lost darling. She was nowhere on board! The negro boatmen were called, and questioned with rifles at their heads, but they all declared with trembling earnestness that they had seen no girl on board.

Tim Rose was astonished, but not quite satisfied ; he took one of the colored men into the skiff, rowed off some distance from the *pirogue*, and subjected him to a searching examination, telling him he should be shot if he hesitated to disclose the whole truth, and promising protection and reward if he revealed the whereabouts of 'Ginia Rose.

"What is your name, boy ?" said Tim.

" Peter, sah."

" Would you like to be a free man ?"

" I reckon," answered the slave, with a light in his countenance which shone even through his terrible fright.

" What did your master do with the little girl?" questioned Tim.

" Fo' God, I dunno nothin' 'bout de gal. Didn't see no gal."

"Where was your master all night ?"

" In de *pirogue*, sah."

" Didn't he go ashore ? "

" No, sah ; didn't go out de boat last night."

" Nor before starting this morning ?"

" No, sah ; didn't go out no time."

" If you are lying, you are a dead nigger," said Tim ; "but you seem to be telling all you know. Let us go back, men, and put the boy on board. It's mighty strange what became of 'Ginia." On

returning to Freeman's boat, Tim exclaimed with
a tone and manner not to be mistaken, "Tom
Freeman, if you carry off my sister's child, you
die."

"Before God," replied Freeman, "I have not
seen my child since I parted with her yesterday at
your father's house."   Freeman was evidently as
much surprised as her uncle at the disappearance
of the child, and after once more assuring himself
that 'Ginia could not possibly be hidden on board,
Tim and his party reluctantly, and with sad disappointment, returned to Shawneetown.

CHAPTER II.

A T the time of our story the United States owned a manufactory of salt at a point twelve miles back of Shawneetown, known as the "Illinois Saline." From those works large quantities of salt were shipped to various points up and down the Ohio, and it was this trade chiefly which had given a start to the town. It was for the purpose of filling up his cargo with this salt, for which New Orleans furnished a ready market, that Summers landed at Shawneetown. A few hours sufficed to get his lading on board; and then, having heard of the mysterious disappearance of 'Ginia Rose, he called on Mrs. Freeman and gave to her the memorandum found on his boat, hoping that it might at some time furnish a clue to the abductor of the child. Immediately afterwards the captain put his boat into the stream, to begin the long voyage to New Orleans.

Soon after dark, before the Tippecanoe had floated many miles down the beautiful river, there came up a very heavy fog ; and as a matter of caution at that stage of water, Summers decided to lie by for a a few hours, till the fog should disperse.   He therefore headed his boat for the shore, and landed on the Kentucky side, opposite the mouth of the Saline River, some eight or ten miles below Shawneetown.   His men went ashore, built a fire at a little distance, and made preparations for supper, while Summers turned in below, where he laid himself down, and soon fell asleep.

How long he had been sleeping he did not know ; but on awakening he became conscious that something unusual was going on.   He heard the sound of oars, which he knew could not be those of his own boat.   He rose hastily, and started for the deck, but the moment his head appeared above the hatchway, he found himself confronted by two men, with heavy pistols in their hands.

" You are our prisoner, Captain Summers," said one of them.   " Your men are all on shore ; you are alone and in our power ; but make no resistance, and you shall not be harmed."

Tom Summers was not the man to do a foolish thing.   He saw that resistance was useless, and he submitted.   There was something in the voice of the man who had addressed him which sounded familiar, though the dress and appearance of the men were strange; but he made no reply. Without a word, he returned below, leaving the deck in the possession of his captors. The measured stroke of oars told him that his boat was being towed by some other craft, and after some time he felt a slight, sudden shock, and knew that the boat had touched the shore.

Captain Summers had already realized that he was in the hands of the robbers of Cave-in-Rock; and that the recent accounts of the depredations of the river pirates who made this cave their headquarters were but too well founded. After the boat was made fast he was approached by a number of armed men, who, telling him he would not be harmed, bandaged his eyes and led him on shore.

Summers had often landed at Cave-in-Rock, and he soon felt sure, from the closeness of the air, that he had entered the cavern. When he had proceeded but a little way he was placed in a large basket, or cage, and felt himself drawn up to a higher apartment. From this point two men conducted him through devious ways, to an inner chamber of the cavern, unbandaged his eyes, placed a lighted lamp and food before him, and telling him to remain in that place at his peril, bade him good-night.

By the time Summers had completed his meal,

which was not only abundant but excellent, a man appeared from an inner apartment of the cavern, bearing a rude mattress and a little bedding, — of which very little, indeed, was necessary. He laid them down near Summers, and addressed him as follows : —

"Captain Miner sends his compliments to Captain Summers, and says that he will do himself the honor of calling upon his guest in the morning."

"And who might Captain Miner be?" inquired Tom.

"It is my business to give you the captain's orders," said the man, "not to answer questions. Good night, Captain." And so saying, he disappeared.

The man was evidently a foreigner, most probably a Spaniard ; but he wore the appearance of a man of the world, and spoke English very well, though with something of a foreign accent.

When he was alone Summers lifted the iron lamp which had been left with him, and proceeded to an inspection of his underground quarters ; but seeing that the oil was nearly exhausted, he prudently used the remaining light in adjusting his bed, and laid down. It need not be said that he did not sleep, — his position was not favorable to the approach of the drowsy god, — but being alone, and, as he supposed, out of the hearing of all others, he very naturally talked to himself : —

"This is a pretty scrape for the captain of the Tippecanoe to be caught in! This is what comes of knowing too much, and of not believing what is told one. I have seen Cave-in-Rock twenty times at least, and I knew that there *used* to be robbers here ; but that Tom Summers has been taken captive by them, has lost his boat and his liberty together, without any chance to show fight, is more than any man in Vincennes will believe ! I hardly believe it myself.

"That voice upon the boat sounded to me very much like — but it couldn't be his. When did he learn the bends of the river all the way to Orleans?"

And so, with vain surmises as to the identity of the robber captain, and bitter regrets for his carelessness in allowing all his men to leave him, he spent the night. Some time towards morning he fell asleep, in which condition he remained until awakened by the entrance of his visitor of the night before, with his breakfast and a light.

Setting down before Summers a good breakfast, smoking hot, the man said, —

"Captain Miner sends his compliments to Captain Summers ; and, if acceptable, will visit him in the course of the forenoon."

" Tell Captain — Miner ? "

" Yes, Captain Miner."

" Tell your captain he is just the man I want to see," said Tom.

The man took up the empty lamp, left the fresh one burning, and departed without a word. On examining the lamp Tom saw that there was barely oil enough to last while he took his breakfast : so he hastened his meal, poured the little remaining oil into a cup-like depression in the rocky floor of his prison, and blew out the flame.

In about an hour two men came to the opening passage which led to his prison, bearing a light. One of them approached Summers, while the other retired, leaving the place in total darkness.

"Captain Summers," said the new-comer," you and I are strangers. Nothing I could say to you would justify my proceeding in your eyes: I shall not make the attempt. But as it is solely owing to my interposition that you have not lost your life as well as your boat, you will perhaps permit me to explain to you something of your prospect for future liberation. First, then, your liberation depends upon yourself. You have shown yourself a man of sense, as I know you to be. Had you made useless resistance, you must have perished. I say *must:* you will understand *why*, Captain

Summers. When your boat and its lading have been disposed of, and our own safety has been assured, you will be set at liberty. In the mean time you will be made as comfortable as our condition and ability will permit. For the fulfilment of this promise rely upon Captain Miner, who knows how to entertain his friends and punish his enemies. But mind, Captain Summers, no resistance, and no attempt to escape!"

"Answer me one question," said Tom, when his jailer had concluded. "Isn't your real name Leyba?"

"Captain Summers," said the other, "such a question as that among gentlemen is exceedingly rude, and is not fairly entitled to an answer. But I answer you on the honor of a man,—No!"

"Well, Captain," said Tom, "I am your prisoner; and I can do no better than to accept your terms."

Captain Miner then briskly clapped his hands; the man with the light approached near enough to show the way, and the robber captain, bidding Tom a polite "Good morning," retired.

In a few hours food and light were brought as before. This time, after the bearer had retired, Summers poured out nearly all of the oil in his lamp into the little pit where he had emptied the other; and when his evening meal was brought, he did the same thing.

Some time after he had eaten the last meal, Summers laid down for sleep, but was roused by the sound of distant music. He listened attentively. The sounds came with gentle echoes through the many avenues of the cavern; and while he strained his ears to catch the notes of this weird music, two men came to him with a message :—

"Captain Miner's compliments to Captain Summers: would be pleased to see him in the banquet-room."

Summers permitted himself to be blindfolded without a word, and was led away, through various windings, to a long avenue, opening into a large, high-arched cavern. Near the entrance to this apartment he was received by the robber captain and conducted to a seat, and he observed that while the whole cavern was brilliantly lighted, the little alcove in which the chief and himself were seated, was purposely kept in deep shadow.

The scene which met the eyes of Summers, as he looked over the lighted cavern, filled him with astonishment. There was a vast hall-like room, large enough apparently, to contain a hundred persons. The floor was quite even and nearly level; and the sides, though rough and uneven in general form, were ornamented with groups and clusters of natural crystals of spar; while from the roof here and there hung sparkling stalactites in great variety and profusion. Around the sides of the cavernous hall at various points, lamps were suspended from the rocky walls; and across the room, just before Summers and the robber captain, was extended a long table, loaded with abundant and apparently luxurious food. In the further end of the apartment sat a young man thrumming a guitar; while in the middle space of the room a number of men and women were gayly dancing. To Tom Summers all these people wore a foreign aspect. The women were dark in complexion,— Portuguese or Spanish, he decided; and the men were evidently of the same nationality. The few words he heard spoken appeared to be Spanish.

After Summers had viewed this apparently happy scene for some time, wondering that such men as these appeared to be could be pirates, Captain Miner beckoned to a young man at the table, who immediately poured wine, and placing the glasses upon a tray, handed them to his captain. Presenting the tray to Tom, he said, —

"Captain Summers, here's that you may never meet a worse man than Captain Miner!"

"I drink that," said Tom, and drank his glass. Not knowing just how bad a man Captain Miner might prove to be, he could safely drink to the hope that he should meet no worse. But he observed that the robber captain only put the wine to his lips, and set it down without tasting. Summers felt tempted to repeat his question of the evening before; but contented himself with the attempt to determine in the dim light around him if the pirate captain were not in fact his passenger, Leyba. The man was evidently disguised; and though his voice much resembled that of Leyba, he spoke with such a foreign accent that Summers was unable to fully satisfy himself on the question; indeed he said but little. After Summers had witnessed the dance for half an hour, he was led back to his own apartment. But before his eyes were again bandaged, he observed several pots of paint, designed, as he suspected, for repainting the Tippecanoe.

When Summers had reached his quarters in the cavern, his conductors unbandaged his eyes, put the lamp by his side, and left him alone. This time his lamp was better supplied with oil than formerly; and after waiting until all was still, Tom took his pocket knife, and using it as a spoon patiently transferred the oil which he had saved into the lamp, and to his great satisfaction found it full. He reduced its flame as much as possible by depressing the wick, placed it in a little alcove in the rock, to conceal its light from any who might be guarding him, and then lay down as if for sleep.

But Captain Summers gave no sleep to his eyes that night. He patiently waited until the distant music had ceased, and long after the faintest echoes had died away. Then, taking off his shoes, to make no noise, he carefully scrutinized his prison throughout all its length and breadth. It was simply a kind of grotto, hollowed out by some unknown agency in the solid limestone rock. There were stalactites and other curious modellings of Nature, which at other times might have engaged his attention; but he was looking for something of far greater present interest. In the most distant part of his prison, high up in the wall he perceived a crevice in the rock, to which, with some difficulty, he climbed. His light was too dim to penetrate the darkness beyond; but, determined to regain his liberty if possible, he entered the fissure, and followed it. It led him to a yawning opening in the rocks, and far down in the darkness he heard the sound of waters. At one point he thought it possible to cross the abyss, and with cautious clambering he reached the spot. Here he hesitated. Any misstep would probably be instant death. He took up a bit of loose stone and dropped it into the cleft; but in that movement the lamp slipped from his grasp, and all was darkness. As he stood still, almost horror-stricken, the falling stone sent reverberations of sound through the cavern, and fell with a dull plunge into the waters below. Hazardous as appeared the attempt, he was about to make an effort to descend, when he saw, almost over his head, but beyond the dangerous opening in the rock, a few dim, twinkling lights. They were stars, shining in their native heaven, and seen through a cleft in the rock. With the cautious movements of a man trained to difficulty, he slowly felt his way across a narrow part of the fissure, and in ten minutes more had succeeded in crossing the barrier, climbing the cleft rock to the top, reaching the outer world, and once more breathing the air of liberty.

It was now midnight. Tom Summers had boated night and day long enough to read the hour by the familiar stars. After some reflection he resolved to proceed down the river, not following its bends, but keeping as near a straight course as possible, in the hope of overtaking the Tippecanoe, which he had no doubt had been sent on her way to the South. At the end of the third day, after a laborious journey over hills, through swamps, and across bayous, he reached the mouth of the Ohio. Here he found no means of crossing; and lying down, chilled and nearly exhausted, he awaited the return of daylight.

About midnight the attention of the weary traveller was aroused by strange unwonted sounds, which appeared to come from the river; they resembled the measured and repeated soughing of some huge beast. Presently he saw fire approaching in the direction whence the sounds proceeded, and he heard a regular beating sound upon water, like the rapid but very powerful dash of oars. Tom Summers was not a man to be frightened, but that he was very much astonished could not be denied. It soon occurred to him that this must be one of those wonderful steamboats of which he had heard rumors, but none of which had heretofore been seen on the Ohio. On came the monster, lashing the waters to foam, and breathing fire and smoke through iron nostrils. On reaching the confluence of the rivers, she rapidly and gracefully rounded to, as if possessed of volition, and in a few minutes more was lying quietly by the shore.

The strange craft proved to be the New Orleans, the first steamer ever built west of the Alleghanies. She had been detained at the falls of the Ohio some time by low water, and was now taking advantage of a recent rise in the stream. As no wood was to be had along the river, only as it was cut for the occasion, she had landed here for the purpose of cutting dry wood from piles of accumulated drift.

Going aboard the steamer, Summers found an old acquaintance in the person of Captain Jack, the pilot ; and although the boat was carrying only freight, he had no difficulty in obtaining passage to New Orleans. His story was considered marvellous in the extreme ; and probably nothing but the character for veracity given of him by Captain Jack saved him from the suspicion of Munchausenism, as all supposed that the robbers of Cave-in-Rock had disappeared long before.

Early on the next morning the steamboat started on her voyage, making nearly a hundred miles before night. At nightfall a heavy fog arose, and it was determined to lie by for the night at a small island, some distance below the little town of New Madrid on the west bank of the Mississippi. Several keel-boats and flat-boats were moored to the mainland some distance below the steamer, — also detained by the fog. The early hours of the night were spent in getting wood from a drift-pile; and as the fog did not abate, all hands then turned in for sleep.

CHAPTER III.

EARTHQUAKES.

ABOUT two o'clock in the morning after the New Orleans was moored at the island below New Madrid, the sleepers were aroused and startled by a tremendous shock, which shook the boat from stern to stem, and filled the astonished voyagers with horror.*   In another moment the river rushed violently from beneath the boat, and the mud bottom bounded up against the frail craft; the returning waters came rushing up their channels in huge waves, bearing the steamer down the stream with a violence which threatened instant destruction.

Loud, hissing noises were heard from the shore; huge trees, shaken from their position, tumbled down, whirling their vast branches into the boiling flood.   The boats which lay further down the river were torn from their moorings, and swept with frightful speed down the roaring flood; many of

* This account of the earthquake is historically true and correct. (1811.)

them were dashed to fragments against the shore. The little island where the steamer had lain burst asunder, and a huge column of sand was blown out by the sulphurous vapors which rushed through the vent into the lurid air. The wild water-fowl which had been sleeping by hundreds in the eddies, flew about, shrieking their terror; and the wife and children of the captain of the steamer joined the affrighted cry.

As the effects of the first shock subsided, all haste was made to raise steam on board the boat. The river continued to run in a direction opposite to its usual course; and scarcely half an hour elapsed ere the agitated earth was heaving with another terrible throe. The second shock, though not so violent as the first, was accompanied by an increase of horrors. The whole earth seemed to be thrown into progressive waves. Vast fissures were opened, pouring out steam and sulphurous vapors, and — as it was afterwards learned — overwhelming vast bodies of land with sand. The river margin sunk several feet for a distance of many miles up and down the river, leaving the village of New Madrid, formerly high ground, below highwater mark; and a large district of the interior suffered similar depression.

Earthquake shocks continued at intervals until

morning. when the steamer continued her difficult course down the river. The morning was one of terrible gloom, and the atmosphere wore a sulphuric hue, as if sympathizing with the earth. About sunrise the Father of Waters broke down the barrier which had been raised by the upheaved earth, and came rushing impetuously down, bearing upon his waves the boats which had escaped the night before. The steamer's engine enabled her to offer partial resistance to the current, but the flat-boats and keel-boats shot by like arrows. Several of them were dashed to pieces on the buried logs which the heaving earth had thrown from their long repose in the river bottom.

For several days succeeding, there were slight agitations of the river, indicating that the earth had not yet regained its quiet; and on landing at the Chalk Banks, it was learned that even so far from the centre of disturbance the shocks had been sufficiently violent to excite great alarm. After the danger was apparently past came the time for an interchange of sentiments and opinions among the men upon the boat, as she passed rapidly on her way to New Orleans.

"Captain Jack," said Tom Summers, approaching the pilot with an expression which indicated a much stronger disposition to express his own views than to obtain those of his old friend, — "Captain Jack, what do you suppose is the matter with the earth ?"

"Why, Captain Summers," said the pilot, "we have had an awful earthquake : that's all I know about it."

"But what makes 'em ?" said Tom.

"I don't know, and I don't believe anybody knows."

"But, Captain Jack, I think nothing happens without a cause — and earthquakes have a cause. Now if this earth turns round on her centre every twenty-four hours, it must get on a strain; and it seems very natural it should bust up some-times."

"Yes, that's so, Tom; but why don't we have earthquakes all the time ?"

"Why don't the fly-wheel of that engine bust up? Fly-wheels do bust when we don't look for it. Anything on a strain must break *sometime;* and no man can tell when it is coming. I guess it is so with earthquakes."

Tom's philosophy brought a smile from Captain Jack, and a laugh from the men standing by. But the keel-boat philosopher continued his talk all the same, reiterating it day by day.

The steamer continued on her novel journey,

and reached New Orleans without further accident, the tremors of the earth occurring at intervals, though with less violence during the remain-
der of the voyage.

CHAPTER IV.

THE TIPPECANOE. — A CHILD'S RELIGION. — THE
CAVE.

SOME weeks after the arrival of the first steamer at New Orleans, Tom Summers was standing
on the levee, watching the approach from above of
a large, new, brightly painted keel-boat, which, not
withstanding its gay color and the word "Louisiana," painted upon its sides, he thought closely
resembled a certain other keel-boat he had known.
Indeed, he was ready to "take his Bible oath"
that the true name of the craft was Tippecanoe.
He kept his own counsel, however, and awaited
further developments. As soon as the boat was
landed, a gentleman closely wrapped in a cloak
came off, leading a young female whose form and
face were also studiously concealed, called a carriage which was near, and entering without a
word, was rapidly driven away. The curiosity of
Summers prompted him to watch the direction
taken by the carriage, but his interest in the keel-
boat interfered, and the latter feeling prevailed.
After several men had gone ashore, Tom stepped

on board, and finding the cargo composed of salt, corn and whiskey, he approached the man who seemed to have the command, and asked,—

"What is Vincennes whiskey worth?"

The man appeared startled: and after a little hesitation replied that the whiskey was not for sale.

"Well, stranger," said Tom, "how much for United States Saline salt?"

"The salt is sold, sir," said the man.

"Well, mayhap you'll sell that Indian corn?"

"The whole cargo is consigned to a house in this city," said the other.

"Oh, it is!" said Tom. "Well, stranger, what will you take for the boat?"

The man addressed turned his back in apparent confusion, and went to the other end of the vessel, while Tom proceeded into the city, for the purpose of taking the proper legal steps to recover his property, and to secure the robbers.

An hour after, when Summers returned with the proper officers, not a soul was to be found on board. The birds had flown.

A few days sufficed for the reclamation of his boat by legal process, for the sale of the cargo, and for taking on board a load suited for the Western market. The word "Louisiana" was effaced from the side of the boat, and "Tippecanoe" restored to its wonted place. A crew of Western men was soon found; and Captain Summers started on his return voyage up the Mississippi.

If Tom Summers had obeyed his curiosity instead of his interest, and had followed the carriage which conveyed from his boat the mysterious personages whom he saw depart, he might have seen them alight at a monastery in the suburbs of the city; as thither they went with all speed. The gentleman rang the gate-bell, and was admitted with his charge; and the carriage was driven away.

"I have brought you my daughter, according to our arrangement," said the man, "and I confide her to your motherly care and protection. She's dear to me as the apple of my eye; and I trust her to you as a most precious jewel."

"You have done well," said the woman addressed, "as you thereby shut out the darkness of this world, and let in the light of a better."

"I leave you the amount necessary for six months, Sister Naomi," said the man; "and should you desire to communicate with me this paper contains my address. Remember! she writes to none; and no one outside your house sees her but myself."

The man kissed his daughter (as he called her)

with manifest emotion, bade the good sister fare-well, and departed.

"What is your name, my child?" said Sister Naomi, as she removed the girl's cloak and hood, and looked into her bright blue eyes.

"My name is Virginia Rose," said the beautiful child, "but everybody calls me 'Ginia."

"Sit down, my child; you must be tired," said Sister Naomi, placing a seat for her. "How old are you, Virginia?"

"I am twelve years old, ma'am; and I am tired doing nothing!"

"Strange!" said the good Sister; "so old, and yet such native simplicity. Have you ever heard of God?"

"Oh, yes; we have God in Illinois. My mother taught me to pray to him."

"And the Holy Child Jesus?" said the Sister.

"Yes,—the Son of God."

"And the Holy Mother of God?" continued the Sister.

"My mother taught me that God was the father of *all*," said the child. "How could he have a mother?"

"Poor child!" said the good Sister, clasping her hands in pity. "Behold this image of the Child Jesus in the arms of the Blessed Virgin."

The child examined the small sculpture with a curious eye, and with doubtful hesitation inquired,—

"Do people pray to such images as this?"

"They pray to God and the Virgin through their images," said the Sister.

"My mother taught me that all graven images are abominable," said the child.

At this reply Sister Naomi gave up the argument in despair; and telling her charge that her mother was a heretic, ended the first lesson.

The backwoods girl soon proved to her instructors that, instead of being entirely unlearned, she had, in their opinion at least, learned too much. However, as she was to remain in the convent school, perhaps for several years, Sister Naomi hoped that time and a rigid discipline would exterminate the germs of a false religion which had been implanted in her mind by a heretic mother.

The sweet and kindly disposition of Sister Naomi's beautiful ward soon endeared her to all who had any intercourse with her. They told her that they did not know such girls as she grew in the woods of Illinois; and with affectionate playfulness asked where she had found those big eyes of blue, that golden hair, that pink and pearl complexion; did they grow on trees in Illinois? Especially they wondered how such affectionate obedience, such winning cheerfulness, could spring up "among the savages!" No bird was more blithe than this rosy lipped girl; and her rippling notes of sweetness filled all her words with melody. Heretofore her education had been limited to the merest elements; but Sister Naomi found the child so ready and apt a pupil as to make it a pleasant task to give her instruction; and her stay at the Sisters' school soon gave promise of rapid progress in all they essayed to teach — except their religion. They declared the child was a born heretic.

After a long and tedious voyage against the strong current of the muddy Mississippi, and through the more gentle waters of the Ohio, Captain Summers again made his cable fast to the shore in front of the promising village of Shawneetown. Here, after disposing of his cargo to the people of the village, he determined to enjoy a few days' repose, and to wear the laurels he had won by his wonderful adventures at Cave-in-Rock. The reports which had been given of the loss of the Tippecanoe and the disappearance of her captain, by the boatmen who had been on shore at the time, and who had found their way back on foot by the Kentucky shore, had excited the greatest wonder; and Tom's account of his captivity and escape now had made him a hero in the people's eyes. His story was repeated again and again in the little town ; and after a few days the excitement ran so high that an expedition was planned against the robbers, under the joint command of Summers and Dan Rose, the frontiersmen. Summers' division was to consist of his boat's crew, together with all the boatmen who could be assembled at short notice ; these were to go in the Tippecanoe by water ; and Rose was to go down by land with his party, consisting of ten or twelve white men and a few friendly Indians. Summers made a rude map, showing the position of the opening by which he escaped, and so impressed its location upon the mind of Rose that he felt confident he could find it without difficulty at night.

After arranging the order of attack, both branches of the expedition left the village about noon, so as to reach the cave about midnight. They were to communicate with each other a mile above the cave, where the Tippecanoe was to land for the purpose.

Dan Rose had not proceeded far with his command before he began to fear that they had undertaken a much more difficult task than had been imagined ; and as the party proceeded he called their attention to the matter : " If we were after twenty· or thirty redskins in the brush, or even in a swamp," said Rose, "we should stand some chance of drawing a sight on them; but how are we to get at them fellows in their underground block-house? Suppose Tom Summers and his men should get possession of the outer cave, and the robbers should let down their big limestone stopper, and close the bung-hole up? No 'coon in a green gum-tree was ever safer than they would be."

"Smoke 'em out," said some one in reply.

"It can't be done," said Rose.

"Starve 'em out," said another.

"Why, according to Tom's theory they have fodder enough for a year," said Rose.

"Wall 'em in," said an old man, who was a kind of jack-stonemason. This suggestion was received with a hearty laugh from all the company.

"Let us *coax* 'em out, father," said Tim Rose; "and when they vacate, we can take possession."

"Rather a bright idea, Tim," said the father. "Tom Summers' boat will make good bait, and we'll make the proposition to Tom when we meet."

This was unanimously voted to be good policy, and the party moved on with vigor. At sunset they had reached a somewhat noted locality, known then and since as Lead Hill. From this place the Indians had long been in the habit of procuring material for their bullets, though the metal procured by the simple process then in use among them, was a compound much resembling silver in appearance. While crossing over this rather singular hill, the party came upon a rude furnace for smelting the ore. It stood contiguous to an old log-hut, which, after reconnoitring and finding unoccupied, some of the party entered and examined. In this place they found apparatus for coining, and portions of the base metal in various stages of preparation up to the finished "bogus." coin. Everything appeared to have been left as if suddenly abandoned. The crucible in the furnace contained a portion of the reduced ore, and the fire beneath appeared to have burned out within a few weeks for the want of some one to supply the fuel which was lying ready prepared.

"Bogus fact'ry," said Tim.

"Ugh!" said the Indians.

"Hush, men," said old Dan Rose, "we are now within sound of their rifles. Nine miles more will bring us to the cave. Round yonder point runs the trail. We leave that to the right and make for the river. Put in fresh priming, pick your flints, and keep a sharp look-out."

The men were all too well trained in backwoods

warfare to require a repetition of this caution. They proceeded noiselessly through the woods, and reached the rendezvous on the river about ten o'clock, and finding the Tippecanoe not yet there, they sat down and patiently awaited its arrival.

Tom Summers and his boatmen had also canvassed the probable success of the undertaking. Lynch, a Kentuckian, who had joined the expedition at Shawneetown, swore that " five good riflemen from 'Kentuck' could defend the cave against all creation."

After many opinions, *pro* and *con*, Summers suggested that by keeping the robbers from the river in front, they might be picked off with a rifle as they attempted to obtain water from the rear of the cavern where he had made his escape. This was considered at least plausible by all hands.

Tom Summers was a native politician, and when the mode of attacking the cave was settled he introduced the new kind of boats as a subject of conversation, and finally propounded his ideas of " co'poration," — a favorite subject of discussion with him.

" I'm agin these smoke-boats," said Tom.

" What's agin 'em ? " asked one of the company.

" What's agin 'em ? Everything is agin 'em. What chance will a good, old-fashioned keel have agin these porposes ? "

"Well, but Tom, ain't they good for the country?"

"Ain't *we* a part of the country?" replied Tom. "'Tain't no justice to ruin one class of men for the sake of another class."

"Them's my sentiments ezactly," said a Tennessean.

"Well, Tom," said Lynch, "we will *all* have to build steamboats, that's all. Good bye, settin' pole!"

"Can *you* afford to build one?" said Tom. "Can I? No, these things cost too much money, and they must be built by these blasted co'porations."

"What's your objection to co'porations, Tom?"

"'Cause they have no souls, nor bodies either to signify; sue one of them for an honest debt and it ain't thar. The *company* hasn't got anything, though every man of it has his pocket full of Spanish dollars. But that's *private property*, they say. Ain't they the men that made the debt? and don't all the profits go into their private pockets? Let 'em be made to pay their debts out of their private pockets. Then I'm agin the whole breed."

"Them's my sentiments, ezactly," said the Tennessean.

"Captain Summers," interposed Lynch, who

was at the helm, " yonder is the mouth of the
Saline ; hadn't we better land, and lie by till ten
or 'leven o'clock ? "

"Good idea, Lynch ; throw her bow in and let
her come round."

The boat was accordingly brought to shore,
where she remained until about ten o'clock, when
she was to be dropped down to the place of rendezvous, a mile above the cave.

While Summers and his men are waiting for the
time to arrive, let us describe the good keel-boat
Tippecanoe, and the class to which she belonged,
and something of the race of hardy boatmen who
are unknown to the present generation.

In general appearance, the keel-boats of sixty
years ago resembled the more modern canal-boat.
The keel was very long and very narrow, and so
shaped as to combine the greatest floating capacity
with the least resistance to the water.   The bow
was rather sharp and considerably greater in length
than breadth ; but the curvature was soon lost in
parallel sides which continued equidistant the entire
length of the boat.   The stem resembled the bow,
but as a rule, was less sharp.   The hull was so
placed upon this keel as to expose some twelve or
fourteen inches of the keel on each side of the
boat, running its entire length.   These projecting

sides rose but little above the water, were planked over, and "cleated" with cross foot-holds for the boatmen, who propelled the boat by placing their "setting poles" upon the river bottom near the stem of the boat, fixing one end against the shoulder and pushing the boat from under them as they walked towards the stern. The men upon the opposite sides worked in pairs, so that an even pressure was maintained on both sides of the boat. But in the deep and turbid waters of the Mississippi, the setting pole was not available. There the "cordell" took the place of the pole. This was a long, light rope, which was generally used by fastening it to some tree or other firm body as far above as the cordell would reach, and then pulling on the other end in the boat. It was slow and laborious work, and it required several months of this arduous toil to propel a keel-boat from New Orleans to the mouth of the Ohio River.

The hull of the keel-boat looked somewhat like the modern ironclad gun-boats, but was less acute in the angle of its sides. On each side, near the centre was a large sliding door for convenience in loading and unloading, and on top a hatchway, by which the boatmen communicated with the interior. The rudder, at the stern, had its steering arm extended along near the deck, so that the steersman generally guided the boat with the lever between his knees.

But the Tippecanoe was almost an exception among keel-boats. She had been built at Vincennes under Summers' own supervision, and with all the improvements which had been suggested to him by his long experience and practical good sense. It was no ordinary event for the little town, when the Tippecanoe, named from the then recent battle between the Indians and General Harrison, started on her long voyage to New Orleans, with Tom Summers in command, and the boatmen singing the well-known refrain : —

> " Hard upon the hickory oar,
>   She moves too slow;
>   Time we were at Shawneetown,
>   Long time ago."

On reaching the place of rendezvous, Summers found Dan Rose and his men in waiting. After some conference between the parties, it was decided that, as the night was dark, it would be necessary for Summers to go with the land party, to avoid the danger of not being able to find the rear opening to the cavern. Lynch therefore took command of the boat ; and after giving the land party half an hour's start, the Tippecanoe was put into the current and permitted to float.

When the shore party reached the vicinity of the cave, Summers was perplexed to find that what he had described as a hill in the rear of the cavern now appeared to be a hollow or depression, as compared with the ground around it. No fissure in the rock was to be found, and the whole contour of the surface appeared to be changed. He first thought he must have missed the locality. But one of the Indians declared that there used to be a hill, and an opening in the rock at that very spot. A messenger was sent around to communicate with the other party. He returned with word that the cave was deserted. The party from the boat had cautiously landed some distance above, and now had possession of the outer cavern.

Rose and his men joined the others in the cave, and proceeded to examine it by the light of the torches, which were already burning.

Boxes and barrels were lying around, very much as Summers had seen them before. But they did not appear to have been in any manner disturbed for a considerable length of time. The central opening, which communicated with the rooms above, was not closed ; the heavy stone which Summers had seen hanging over it appeared to have fallen, and was lying at one side of the opening. The large basket, which had been used for ascending and descending, was hanging from its suspending pulley above. Summers seized the rope and was about to climb, but one of the Indians called him back, and placing a hat and coat upon a pole thrust them up through the opening. He had supposed that they might be fired on ; but all was silence.

Tom now boldly entered the opening, torch in hand, followed by Rose, Tim, Lynch, and others. The mouldy remnants of a feast which had never been eaten were lying upon a table ; lamps were hanging around, burnt out for want of oil ; and a tray of glasses filled with untasted wine was on a small stand ! But the avenues which had led to the inner cavern had disappeared. The rock had fallen from above in vast masses, and closed all connection between the cave and the outer world forever. Perhaps in the midst of gay festivity, perhaps in the hour of music and dancing ! Who could say ? Not a soul was left to tell the tale.

The men who had come to execute vengeance could not now avoid sympathy for the dead. He who hath said "Vengeance is mine," had sent the earthquake to do His will, and these hardy men felt that they were in the presence of Eternal Justice. They left the sparkling wine untouched in the glasses, and descended to the room below. Here they secured such articles as were of value ; and putting them on board the Tippecanoe, prepared to return in the morning to Shawneetown. •

Next day, bright and early, the boat was stemming the current of the Ohio. The river was at such a stage as to render the setting-pole of little value, and recourse was had to the cordell. A long line was sent ashore and made fast to a tree at its full length above the boat ; and then by dint of vigorous pulling at the other end by the men on board, the boat was brought up to the point of attachment, made fast, and the rope sent ahead to another tree, as before. Occasional help from the setting-pole, the number of men on board, and the absence of lading, made the labor comparatively easy ; and the Tippecanoe landed at Shawneetown before sunset.

CHAPTER V.

GOVERNMENT AT THE CIRCUMFERENCE. — DIVIDED COUNSELS.

ON the night after the return of the Tippecanoe, Summers, Lynch, the Roses, and others of the late expedition, together with several of the good people of the village, were collected at Wilson's tavern to relate or to listen to the news of the day, and, some of them at least, to partake of the landlord's Vincennes whiskey.

Tom Summers was by common consent permitted to give "official" account of the recent expedition to Cave-in-rock. Of course the story was well told. He had not been with the land party however; and when Tim Rose exhibited a counterfeit dollar from Lead Hill, as a sort of text to his discourse, Tom was compelled reluctantly to hold his peace. After both had told their stories and answered the inquiries which arose, the conversation turned upon the subject of war with England, a declaration of which was now confidently looked for.

"Captain Summers, what do you expect about

the war?" said a Tennessee boatman mentioned in a former chapter.

"I expect that the sooner it comes, the better," said Tom.

"Them's my sentiments ezactly," said the Tennessean.

"I'm agin the British havin' Canada," said Tom. "It's a splendid country, and ought to belong to us; and if Jim Madison will kick up a war instead of making embargoes on trade, we'll *have* it."

"Ezactly," responded the Tennessean.

Summers was so well pleased with his own patriotism that he paused to order Mr. Wilson to "treat the whole company" at his expense. Mr. Wilson was disposed to draw Summers out farther; and as he filled the glasses with green Vincennes whiskey, he turned to Tom and said:—

"Isn't there danger of our country getting to be too large, Captain Summers?"

"Too large!" replied Tom. "It can't get too large, 'cause its strength is in the circumference. Monarchies git too large, 'cause the strength's is all in the centre. I expect this nation to cover all creation, some day, 'cause it's just naturally bound to spread out."

"Then," said Lynch, "Kaintuck will be right in the centre of the earth—Hurrah!"

"Then there won't be any centre," said Tom. "The people are the government. The people will be everywhere, and in course there can't be any centre."

This proposition was rather too metaphysical for most of Tom's hearers; but the Tennessee boatman thought he understood it perfectly; so he assented as usual :—

"Ezactly; them's *my* sentiments."

Tom Summers continued :—

"There won't be a centre for another reason: There won't be any standin' army. In a monarchy, the standin' army is the centre of gover'ment; but here the people is the army, and they will be everywhere; and in course, then, there can't be any centre."

"Ezactly," was the response.

"Boys, take a little more!" exclaimed Tom.

"Them's my sentiments," said the Tennessean, at the same time swallowing his second glass of Vincennes.

The conversation now turned upon the lost daughter of Mrs. Freeman. "How about that child?" said Summers, addressing Dan Rose. "We started in such a hurry after them Cave-in-rock gentry that I never got time to ask how the gal got lost. What do you suppose became of her?"

"I have my own suspicions," said the old man, "but it will never do to tell Katy. She is near enough crazy now."

"Think that man, Freeman, got her?" inquired Tom.

Rose slowly shook his head, but made no reply.

"Dan Rose," said Tom, "let me tell you something. Are you sure Freeman went home to Kaintuck?"

"Oh, yes," said Tim, taking up the answer. "I overhauled him way above the Wabash, making for Limestone fast as his niggers could take him. 'Ginia wasn't with him, sure."

"Well, I'll bet he took her to Orleans," said Tom ; "and on that very boat down there, at the landin'. When them Cave-in-Rock men landed her at Orleans, the first man as stepped on shore was wrapped all up in a cloak, and was leading a little gal by the hand. They got into a carriage, and drove off like a hurricane."

"What sort of a looking little gal was it?" asked Tim.

"Could'nt see her face, Tim,—all wrapped up in shawls and veils."

"Father," said Tim, "that child is in Orleans. I always thought that Tom Freeman had got her, somehow : now I know it." Then he added, "If

Freeman's about Limestone, I'll know it. If he isn't I'll know that."

Tim's revolution was taken. He determined to make a trip to Limestone, and learn whether Freeman really returned directly home or not.

"You will waste your time, Tim," said the father, sadly. "Tom Freeman is no doubt at home, and knows no more about the gal than you do. But go if you please."

"Come, boys," said Captain Summers, "let's go aboard: it's time to turn in."

"Ezactly," said the assenting Tennessean. And the company dispersed for the night.

Next morning, when Katy Freeman heard of Summers's story about the persons whom he saw leave his boat in the carriage, the half-closed wounds in her mother-heart were opened afresh. She had become assured that Freeman had not the child. And although it had been intimated that by bare possibility the child might have been stolen by Indians, she rejected this alternative as impossible. Since the battle of Tippecanoe in the preceding November, some bands of savages had evaded the rangers, stolen some horses from the Salt Works, and murdered a whole family, some miles down the river. But she considered the stealing of her child from her side a feat impossible

even to Indians, and had recently settled down in
the belief that 'Ginia must have gone out unper-
ceived for a ramble on the river bank, fallen in,
and drowned.

It was now probable, however, that her daughter
was not only alive, but imprisoned and ill treated,
in a far-off city. The thought was agony, and she
gave way to her feelings in a flood of tears.

Her father attempted to calm her sorrow and
restrain her tears.

" Katy," said the old man, " there's no use cryin'.
God will take care of the little girl. The child has
given you a heap o' trouble always, Katy ; and now
Providence has taken her away. There's no use
cryin', Katy."

The tears fell all the faster. The old mother
then tendered her kind offices.

" Katy, my daughter, I loved my children as
nobody but a mother could : I saw Sam and Johnny
shot down dead before my eyes by the Indians.
But I never shed a tear."

" O mother," said Katy, " if I knew my child
was dead I think it would be a consolation. But
there is a mysterious and tender tie that binds me
to her, and tells me she is still alive. For months
and years I have lived only in 'Ginia ; and I still
feel it in my heart that she is alive and suffering."

"Tut, tut, Katy," said the old man. "For a girl who has been raised on the frontier, as you have, you talk real strange. A woman's child is no more than any other little one she's nursed and loved. A woman wouldn't know her own child any more'n an animal. I remember a hen that hatched an eagle's egg, and clucked kindly to the young one 'till it tore her eyes out."

"Father," responded Katy, "don't talk so! Often as my child was stolen, long as she was from my sight, I never for a moment forgot her cry; I would know it in darkness and in blindness. I know the sweet odor of her breath; I knew her peculiar and gentle touch upon my cheek; I know her gentle breathing, unlike any other's. Could I forget her sweet prattle as she grew, or when she first lisped the name of mother? And when she walked alone!—no other child had just the step of 'Ginia. None but her mother could love her or mourn for her as I do."

After a moment, she said, "Now I feel that there's some kind of connection between that mysterious memorandum found upon Captain Summers's boat and my lost child: '*Angela with the black woman; known only as Virginia: Limestone to Shawneetown;*' what can this mean but my 'Ginia?"

"O Katy," replied her father, "that is a mere coincidence. What did Summers's strange passenger know of your child?"

Katy's father had already considered this memorandum, and did not feel quite sure it was a mere coincidence; but as it gave no clue to the lost child, he thought best to make light of it.

"Well, well, Katy," said the old man, after a time, "there's reason in all things. Dry your eyes. Your brother Tim is going to take another hunt for the child; and if 'Ginia is to be found this side o' the grave, Tim will find her."

"It's very kind of brother Tim," answered Katy, "but he will not find her. I was too happy—*too* happy—with Freeman away and 'Ginia by me always. Oh, I was too happy! And yet I fondly thought it might last always, and that I might always hear my merry bird about me, and look down into her heart through her clear blue eyes. Oh! 'Ginia, my lost 'Ginia!"

A fresh burst of tears seemed to relieve her for a moment, when she resumed, in a low, subdued tone,—

"I could have borne the long years of coldness and abuse,—the suspicion, the falsehood, the worse than brutal cruelty; I could have borne to be the widow of a living husband; I could have borne the

cruel robbery of my child, sore and repeated affliction as it was ; and I could almost forgive it all for
the depth of maternal love which it kindled and re-
kindled, brighter and brighter, in my heart. Oh,
I could have borne all these if I might at last
possess my heart's jewel in safety. But *this* was
not for me. My cup of bitterness was not yet full.
May the God of the widow and the orphan enable
me to bear my fate!"

A low "Amen!" passed from the lips of her
mother; and the weeper was left alone to the
soothing influence of tears.

In the early part of the ensuing day two keel-
boats were seen coming around the point of land
at the bend of the river below the village, and Tim
Rose made ready to depart, intending to obtain a
passage upon one of the boats. It was possible to
see an approaching boat several miles down the
river from the bank at the landing ; and while Tim
was waiting, an old slave, who had been in the
family for many years, and who had formerly belonged to Freeman, took occasion to call Tim aside,
and speak to him on the subject of his proposed
journey.

"Massa Tim, you gwine all de way back to de
ole place for nothin'."

"Why, Aunt Tabby," said Tim, "how do you know that?"

"I knows it, Massa Tim; I dreamt Missus' child was dead, dat berry night it was tuk away."

"But, Aunt Tabby, I don't believe in dreams."

"I jest *know* Miss Katy's child's dead," said the negress.

"Why, what do you mean, Tab, talkin' that way?" said Tim, with a stern look of inquiry into the face of the slave.

"I doesn't mean nuffin, Massa Tim," said the woman, "but when Aunt Tabby dreams, she dreams."

The old creature had never been suspected of knowing anything of the lost child; but from this moment Tim believed she knew the cause and the manner of 'Ginia's disappearance. The woman had been employed by Freeman to take care of the child, on those occasions when he had stolen it from its mother. And Tim now suspected that Freeman must somehow have secured her aid in getting 'Ginia away. The more he thought of this the more plausible it appeared. How could the girl have been taken out of the house, but by the aid of some one in it? And then Tabby's anxiety to have him give up his expedition, — how was this to be accounted for otherwise?

The boats had now reached the landing, and as Tim was more than ever determined to hunt up Freeman, he went immediately on board and obtained a passage to Limestone.

CHAPTER VI.

A PERPLEXED FRENCHMAN. — A RESCUE. — BACK-WOODS SURGERY.

THE journey of Tim Rose to Limestone and back consumed a month. He found Freeman at home, and learned with certainty that he had returned directly there, after his visit to Shawnee-town, and that he brought no one back with him but his own negroes. Giving up the search in that direction as hopeless, he hastened his return to Shawneetown. At Cincinnati he learned that war had been declared against England, and he was the first to bring the intelligence to the towns below.

When Tim's failure to learn anything of the lost Virginia at Limestone was known, it excited but little surprise. None of the family had any con-fident hope of his success. Old Tabby could not refrain from indulging in an " I told you so, Massa Tim!" So she had, truly. But *then* Tim thought she did so from design : now he attributed it to her superstitious belief in dreams.

The news of the declaration of war was received

with satisfaction, and even with gratification by the people of the town, and indeed, throughout the territory. It was thought that it could not make matters any worse, and in the end must make them better. The Indians on the Illinois River and on the Upper Mississippi had long been hostile, and were committing acts of rapine and murder daily; and it was supposed that the declaration of war would compel them to throw off their disguise, and join the standard of one or the other of the parties. It would also compel the general government to extend protection to the West, where the people despairing of legal protection in many instances, had taken the matter into their own hands.

The military spirit was aroused throughout the territory. Companies of " rangers," chiefly composed of volunteers, were formed, and were soon scouring the country in various directions, on the Illinois and Sangamon rivers, and through the interior from the Wabash to the Mississippi. Dan Rose put himself at the head of a small company of volunteers, and undertook to drive off a band of hostile Indians which had been prowling about, occasionally visiting the settlements in the southern part of the territory, and committing frequent robberies and occasional murders.

In the company of Dan Rose, besides ten or

twelve experienced backwoods riflemen, there were three or four boatmen, — including Summers, Lynch, and the Tennessean already known to the reader, — and a negro belonging to Rose. Tim Rose declined going; he had devoted himself to the continued search for his sister's daughter, and had determined to visit New Orleans for that purpose.

In less than a week after the news of the declaration of war had arrived, Rose and his men were equipped with everything necessary, armed with the deadly backwoods rifle and the hunting-knife, and on their way in search of the savages. In frontier countries, the departure of such a band, on such an expedition, was an event which interested the whole community. There was hardly a family which had not at least a dear friend, if not a father or a brother in that little band. No wonder, then, that there was a general turn-out of the villagers to witness the departure. Mr. Wilson, the patriotic landlord, knocked in the head of a barrel of whiskey, the universal promoter of good feeling, and also of some not quite so good, and bade the volunteers drink "to the destruction of redcoats and redskins." It was the universal rule for men on such expeditions to take no spirits with them (unless for medicine), and the Rangers did ample

justice to Mr. Wilson's Vincennes, as being the last
they would get for some time.

At the close of the first day, Captain Rose's
company had reached the Salt Works, where they
proposed to spent the night.   Here the expedition
was joined by a very valuable little Frenchman
named Lesure.   He had been for years engaged
about the Salt Works, and took extreme pleasure
in detailing various incidents in their history.
During the early part of the night the men were
gathered about the furnace fires, roasting corn,
which was just then "in the milk," and made a
pleasant and wholesome food.   Lesure sat down
in their midst and talked for hours.

"You see, Captain Rose," said he, "we do ver'
leetel like de peoples do.   Ven dey makes de vit-
tal cook, dey poot de wood to de fire ; but ven we
makes de salt cook, de fire must be poot to de
wood, eh ? you see ? "

"You move your furnace from place to place,
wherever there is plenty of wood," responded
Rose.

"Yes, sare, captain, ver' good, ver' good !   Hah,
ha !   And we put de — de — saline watare into
one leetel log, and bring him to the fire.   I tell
you one ver' good joke, captain, 'bout dat leetel
log.   Long time 'go, one Frenchman and one

Yankee cook de salt here. Frenchman 'way up dare, half mile; Yankee down dare, half mile. Frenchman dig ver' deep well; find plenty saline watare; make good pump; put on two horse to pump him, and put one leetel log down to his furnace to bring de watare. Yankee dig well too ; put on pump, and make de one horse pump him, and put leetel log down to his furnace to bring de watare. Ver' well : Frenchman's two horses work ver' hard, his pump work ver' good ; but de leetel log bring only one ver' leetel watare, like my fingare. Ah, ha ! By gar ! what is the mattare ? Frenchman look at de leetel log all over ; lectel log not spill de watare anywhere. Frenchman ver' moche surprise. Put two more horses to de pump, all the same. De leetel log not pour out all de watare, only big as my fingare. Frenchman bear him long time, — six months, — twelve months. Then he go and see Yankee's pump : one horse pump a leetel watare, big as my fingare, den he leetel astonish : go to de Yankee's furnace, Yankee cook heap a' salt, and he leetel log run out big stream. Den Frenchman ver' moche astonish. Den he get mad, and tear up de leetel log from de pump to the furnace. By gar ! what you think ? "

The captain gave no answer, however, for the very good reason that he was fast asleep.

" What *you* tink ? " he continued, now addressing Lynch, who was still awake.

" I think it beats old Kaintuck," said Lynch.

" My sentiments," said the Tennessee boatman.

" I tell you what you tink," said Lesure. " De Frenchman's leetel log and de Yankee's leetel log run cross, like dis," holding up his fingers, one across the other. " De Frenchman's log was on top de Yankee's log ; and by gar ! dere was one big hole bore from Frenchman's log ! De Yankee was too moche for de Frenchman. He make de Frenchman's four hosses pump watare for him, while his one hoss pump for de Frenchman ! *What you tink ?* "

By the time Lesure had finished his story, the Tennessee boatman was the only auditor left awake. He therefore felt himself called upon for a response ; and he answered by echoing the Frenchman's words : —

" What do I think ? "

" Yes, sare.   Yankee was one scoundrel."

" Ezactly."

" One big rogue ! "

" Ezactly."

And then, his feelings rising with his effort at a climax of hard names, the Frenchman added, — now sure that the Tennessean would assent to anything, —

"Yes, sare — he was one — one — one —infernal *Yankee!*"

Whether Lesure thought possible to continue the climax any higher than the word "Yankee" is uncertain. At any rate, any further attempt was cut short by a most inharmonious concert of cow-bells which suddenly broke upon the stillness of the night, and made the forest ring with its discord. The whole party was awake in a moment; but before they had time to form an opinion as to the origin of the noise — though all suspected it to have been produced by Indians — their negro man, Solomon, bounded into their midst on a large, fine horse, with a string of bells around its neck.

"Massa Rose," said Solomon, "I bring you a good hoss and plenty of cow-bells."

"Why, Sol, where in the name of your great namesake did you get these?" inquired Rose.

"Tuk 'em from de Injins, Massa Rose."

"From the Indians, Sol? That story won't do. Tell us where you got the horse and bells," said Rose.

"Tuk 'em from de Injins, Massa, sure as Gospel," responded Sol. "Ye see, I tell you jest how 'twas," he continued, as the company gathered round to hear his story. "When Massa Rose an' de Rangers turn in for de night, I slip ober to de

Saline Creek to ketch some fish; build little fire on
de bank; put on de bait, an' lay down by de fire.
After 'while go to sleep little, and forget to wake
up.   Big Injin come and git straddle o' me, and
say, "*Got you now, nigga!*"   He, he, he!   So he
did got me.   Nebba min', after 'while I got *him*.
'How de do, Injin?' says I.   'Glad to see you.   I
want to see Injin long time: gwine to live wid you
long time ago.'   'Berry good,' say de Injin, 'berry
good.   Git on de hoss, broder nigga, and go wid
Injin.'   Injin den put ole Sol on de hoss and tie
all dese bell roun' his neck, and stuff 'em full ob
leaves, so dey would 'nt ring.   Den Injin 'bout to
git on 'nudder hoss, an' ole Sol stick his heel in de
hoss's flank, an' away he go troo de wood like old
Scratch!   Injin shoot, an' holler like wildcat.
Couldn't hit dis chile in de dark, no how!   Leaves
all come out o' de cow-bells, an' scare de hoss so
bad he run right here, straight.   He, he, he!
Massa Rose, I git you good hoss an' plenty of cow-
bells.   He, he!"

The fellow had secured a good horse and twenty
or thirty bells, worth a dollar apiece..   Henceforth,
Old Sol was a hero; and during the whole expedition never got done talking of his success in out-
witting the Indian.

Dan Rose questioned the negro closely to learn

whether there were other Indians in the neighbor-
hood. Solomon had seen but one. It was nearly
certain, however, that a single hostile Indian would
not venture so near the settlement. Telling the
men to look to their rifles, Rose posted sentinels;
and telling them to be ready to take the trail by
daybreak, laid himself down to sleep.

Before sunrise next morning the rangers had
partaken of their homely breakfast, and started in
search of the savages. Taking old Sol's fishing fire
as a starting point, they traced the Indian's horse
up to the north fork of the Saline Creek several
miles, where they found a camp-fire still burning.
Here it was evident a number of Indians had camped
the night before. A fresh trail, still distinct, led
off from the Creek directly north; and the tracks
of several horses were found in the company.

Rose addressed his men, telling them that the
Indian who lost his horse and bells had, no doubt,
given the alarm, and so prompted the whole band
to hasten out of reach of the settlement as quickly
as possible, for fear of pursuit. He warned them
to be on their guard against surprise, and then
pushed on with all speed in the direction of the
trail. At dark they had reached the borders of a
prairie, without coming in sight of the savages,
though their trail was distinctly seen, leading

across the prairie. Here Rose halted his men.
It was thought that the Indians had doubtless
camped on the other side of the prairie, as they
could not get wood any nearer, and would not be
apt to go further ; and so, after an hour's rest, the
Rangers again commenced their march. The
prairie was about four miles across. Taking their
course by the stars, the men proceeded in silence
until they reached the opposite border of the
prairie. Here, after careful reconnoitring, they
discovered the Indians' camp-fire. The men were
therefore halted, while Rose himself went forward
to more closely examine the position of the savages.
He found them under the bluff bank of a small
creek, where, with the water on one side and the
bank on the other, they had built their fire in such
a manner as to guard against surprise. By stealing
up a bend of the creek, he was enabled to see them
seated round the fire, apparently unsuspicious of
danger. He made them out to be ten in number ;
and distinctly saw by the firelight several scalps
dangling from one fellow's girdle. Two or three
horses were also tethered on the bank.

On returning to his little band of Rangers, Rose
divided them into two parties. They were to approach the creek at a right angle until they came
within a hundred paces, when the two parties were

to diverge, one passing below and the other above the Indians. Rose's party were to fire first; and before the Indians recovered from their surprise, the other party were to pour in their fire.

When the two divisions had reached their positions, a new difficulty arose. The bend of the creek was such that the two parties and the Indians formed the three points of a triangle; and just behind the savages, against the bank of the creek, was seen a white prisoner, bound hand and foot. If the original plan of attack were carried out, this poor fellow was sure to receive the converging fire of both parties. Rose hesitated for a moment. Knowing that the other party would wait for his fire, he adopted an expedient, suggested by memories of his boyhood, to draw the Indians away from their prisoner. Going into the woods a little distance, and capturing a number of lightning bugs, which were flying about in hundreds, he took an empty glass bottle from his pocket, put the living fireflies into it, and corked them up. Then setting the bottle afloat in the creek, he returned to his men and awaited the result. It proved as he anticipated. One after another of the savages left the fire, and approached the water's edge, to see the strange light which was flashing and sparkling in the water. The favorable moment arrived, and Rose commanded his men to fire. Five Indians fell; and before the remaining five recovered from their surprise, the other party of Rangers delivered their fire, and three more fell. The remaining two leaped upon the bank, mounted their horses, and escaped in the darkness. One of these ran by the prisoner as he fled, and struck him a blow upon the head with a tomahawk.

After reloading their rifles, both parties approached to examine the slain. Among the first to reach them was old Solomon, the negro. Taking it for granted that they were all dead, he imprudently ventured into their midst, was dragged down by an old savage while in his very death-struggle, and killed by a single plunge of the knife. Poor Sol! he was only a slave, but he was esteemed and trusted by all who knew him; besides, as legal property in man was acknowledged in Illinois Territory, his death was also "a dead loss of a thousand dollars," as Lynch remarked.

The prisoner had been severely wounded by the tomahawk; his skull was injured, and bleeding badly. After his limbs were loosed, he was laid on a bed of leaves, and Lesure, the Frenchman — who now proved to be something of a surgeon — poured water from the creek upon the wound until the hemorrhage stopped, and then dressed it as well as his means would permit. The prisoner was found to be a young man, about twenty years of age; but as he was stupefied by his wound, could give no account of himself. He appeared, from his dress and other indications, to be a stranger in that part of the State,— if, indeed he was even a Western man ; and his rescuers were perplexed in the attempt to form a definite opinion concerning him.

It was considered futile to follow the Indians who had escaped ; and after posting sentinels out in the darkness the Rangers laid themselves down for repose.

Early next morning, while preparing breakfast, some of the men thought they heard the report of a rifle in the direction of the prairie. A scout was sent to reconnoitre. He found a company of Rangers from Kaskaskia, who were scouring the country from that place to Vincennes on the Wabash. They had seen the trail of Rose's company, but no signs of Indians, though a small band of savages had been reported to them by a scout as having committed a murder near the mouth of the Ohio.

A conference was held between the two companies, after which Rose and a portion of the volunteers with him joined the Kaskaskia company — as that had been organized under the authority of Gov. Edwards, — while Summers and the boatmen prepared to return to Shawneetown.

A litter was made for the wounded young man, which the men carried on their shoulders, relieving each other in turn. The party was two days reaching the Salt Works. The wounded man had unexpectedly so far recovered as to be able to ride on horseback; though, owing to a depression of the skull upon the brain, he was still unable to give a coherent account of himself, or even his name. He was therefore placed on a led horse, and accompanied by the men to Shawneetown, after resting one night at the Salt Works. Lesure did his best to have him left behind to the tender mercy of his primitive surgery; but it was thought best to take him to the town, where he might have the benefit of more skilful treatment.

When they reached town, the Rangers carried their patient, almost as a matter of course, to the house of Dan Rose, — for his good wife added to her many housewifely accomplishments that of being the best nurse in the village. She received him with hospitality and the kindness of a good Samaritan.

It was soon apparent that the stranger had fallen into good hands. His general health was soon restored, and he became to all appearances well; but he remained unconscious of his condition, having apparently forgotten all past events, and had nearly lost the power of coherent speech. The few words which he did say, however, filled his nurse with astonishment. "*Not* Virginia Leyba," he would say, "but 'Ginia Rose."

One day when he had been muttering these words in the presence of Katy Freeman, she turned to him suddenly and asked,—

"Do you know anything of 'Ginia Rose?"

"Sh! don't whisper it," said he.

Then, seeing tears come into her eyes, he said in a low, soft tone, —

"Why, how should *you* know? How strange!"

It was clear to Katy that this young man was muttering the name of her daughter; but how was 'Ginia's fate wrapped up with his? Where had *he* heard her name? and could *he* have had any agency in her abduction? The latter suspicion was banished as soon as formed. The whole appearance and bearing of the man, notwithstanding his unconsciousness, forbade such a conclusion. Kindness and generosity were impressed upon his countenance, and there was a tone of sympathy in his voice when he pronounced the name of

'Ginia which showed him to be animated by a generous emotion. At length the fear that her daughter had shared his captivity with the Indians, and fallen a victim to their cruelty, possessed the mother's heart, and she sought by all the arts of kindness to win the stranger's confidence, and to draw from his clouded mind his knowledge of her lost darling.

After several weeks, it was determined that the wounded man should be trephined, in hope that the operation would remove the pressure of the skull upon the brain, and restore his reason.

The reader is no doubt aware that the instrument with which surgeons usually perform this operation is a small, hollow cylinder of steel, having upon its end teeth resembling those of a saw. With this the surgeon takes out a small button of bone, by rotating the instrument backward and forward upon the skull with his hand. The instrument used by Dr. Reed on this occasion, however, was of a somewhat different kind. It consisted simply of a carpenter's centre-bit and brace. It has been said that true skill consists in adapting the means to the end. If that is true, then was Dr. Reed a man of rare skill; for, putting a shield on the bit to prevent its going too far, he boldly put the brace against his breast, and bored an inch hole through the skull. The effect was wonderful, and its success clearly proved the doctor's skill.

"Where am I?" said the stranger, the moment his brain was relieved from pressure.

CHAPTER VII.

THE WOUNDED MAN'S STORY.

MRS. ROSE and Katy continued their kind attention to the stranger, while the wound inflicted by the rude trephine was healing. Katy exhibited such interest in his welfare that when he had sufficiently recovered to do so with safety, he attempted to gratify her desire to hear the history of his captivity among the Indians, and the events which immediately preceded. Katy, with a woman's prudence, avoided all allusion to the incoherent words which he had spoken, until she could be sure that he possessed some knowledge in relation to her lost daughter.

Beginning with his name, like a sensible man as he was, the young man proceeded :—

"My name, as you already know, is Francis Sinclair. I was born in New Orleans, and lost my father in early life. My mother, who was a pious Catholic, designed me for the Church; and I was accordingly educated for the priesthood. My mother had a brother at St. Louis, on the Mississippi, engaged in mercantile business, who, ever since the death of my father, had urged her to remove to that place. But the difficult navigation of that river, together with my mother's strong desire to be with her son, prevented her acceptance of his invitation. Four months ago, however, he sent her a renewed invitation, stating that he had made arrangements with a good priest in St. Louis to continue my instruction, if that should still be necessary.

"I was now of an age to be able to choose for myself my course in life; and I must acknowledge that the service of the Church was not that choice. I hoped, therefore, that the opportunities of this wild country would favor my desire of entering a field of labor better suited to my taste ; and my urgent solicitation decided my mother to risk the journey, which has .had such a sad termination ! My poor, dear mother fell a victim to the murderous savages. But I will not anticipate.

"My uncle's barge, loaded with merchandise, was lying at the levee; and three days after my mother decided to go to St. Louis, we were on the turbid waters of the Mississippi. On going aboard the barge, we found that we were to have other companions for the voyage beside the captain of the vessel and the French boatmen. These were

Sister Naomi, a nun whom I had known before, and a young girl of some thirteen years, named Virginia — you look very pale, madam (speaking to Katy). Are you ill?"

"Oh, I am better, sir," said she. "Please go on."

Sinclair continued: —

"This fairy creature was named Virginia Leyba. From the first moment of our meeting, it seemed to me that I was dreaming, so like the bright images which had often filled my vision in my dream-hours was this blithe, blue-eyed girl.

"Do not suspect me, my dear madam, of having fallen in love — at least after any ordinary manner — with this child, for she was a child, after all; and yet I loved her because she was a child.

"Well, this bright rosebud, just ready to burst into womanhood, and the good Sister Naomi, were our companions for the voyage. We were more than two months slowly creeping up the muddy river. The boatmen were seldom idle long enough to feel the want of amusement, though they often enlivened the tedium of the voyage by snatches of song, or stories. But we poor passengers were driven to many expedients to vary the dull monotony. Sister Naomi managed for the first month to keep her cheerfulness by giving to her young pupil lessons in literature and in religion. In the former study her progress appeared to me marvellous; but she did not give the good Sister very satisfactory evidence of her devotion to Mother Church. However, her ignorance of Catholic theology was amply atoned for by her wit and girlish philosophy. For my own part, I divided my time between reading to my mother and listening to the voice of Virginia Leyba. After the first month, Sister Naomi seemed to tire of her daily routine of assigning lessons and hearing her pupil recite. She gave up literature, therefore, and confined herself to religious instruction, saying that the child had imbibed such erroneous ideas and opinions from her heretic mother that it would require a good while to exterminate them. 'Oh, yes,' said Virginia to me, laughingly, ' it will require a long, *long* while.'

"Well, after this," continued Sinclair, "Virginia and I enjoyed the golden hours together. We watched the bubbling waters as they hurried by; we admired the gay festoons of pendent moss, as they trailed from the river's bordering trees; we listened to the merry chatter of the paroquet, and the exulting cry of the kingfisher as he rose from the water with his finny prey; we watched the graceful swans, which sometimes floated in the eddies, and dashed the muddy water over their snowy plumage. Whole hours we would sit at the vessel's side, waiting for some unlucky fish to swallow our baited hooks. And at this amusement my companion was far my superior. There really appeared to be a fascination in her touch, so that the fish could not resist the temptation to swallow her bait. My own hook might hang for hours without a nibble; and yet, only let Virginia touch the hook with her fairy fingers, and the charmed barb was sure to bring up its victim.

"One day I called her Virginia Leyba, as usual, when she said, in an undertone, not to be heard by others, '*Not* Virginia Leyba, but '*Ginia Rose.*'

"It appears that another did hear, however, for Sister Naomi, with a voice of reprimand, called her from the other end of the barge. From that moment we were alone together no more.

"The next day my mother took occasion to say that a young man who had devoted his life to the priesthood, as I had, should never permit himself to look twice at a pretty face, even though it were the face of a child; for that the young bud just bursting into beauty is more dangerously fascinating than the full-blown rose. I replied that not I, but my mother, had so devoted me; and that there was that within me which I feared would sadly conflict

with her intentions. I am now thankful that I said
no more, as my poor dear mother is gone forever."

"But my daughter, — my 'Ginia," said his anxious auditor, who could bear no longer. "Does *she*
yet live? Oh, do not tell me she is dead!"

"She escaped when I was made captain; and no
doubt, is still living," replied Sinclair. "But can
it be possible that she is yours?"

A full history of 'Ginia's disappearance was
given, and Sinclair became certain that the kind
nurse who had dressed his wounds, —

> "And with the healing potion poured
> The opiate of a woman's word,"

was the mother of the beautiful creature who had
crossed his path of life so strangely.

Sinclair anticipated his narrative to tell his auditor that 'Ginia and her present guardian, Sister
Naomi, had no doubt arrived safe at St. Louis, and
then resumed : —

"For days and weeks that sad, confiding undertone lingered on my ear, — 'Not Virginia Leyba,
but *'Ginia Rose.'* A new tie had bound me to the
captive bird: that tie was *mystery.* What strange
history was hidden beneath the words?

"I ventured one day to ask her kind guardian
for the girl's history; she replied: 'Her father,
Don Antonio de Leyba, brought her to my care,

and as he trusted me with her instruction, I trusted him with her history. I did not question him.'

" 'But who is Don Leyba ? ' " said I.

" 'A friend to our House, who, having devoted large sums to the Church, has, wisely, no doubt, devoted his daughter to its service.'

"I asked no more questions, but from that moment my resolution was taken. I determined to rescue this young creature, who was formed to be the light and joy of the social world, from her unnatural destination. I could not doubt that there was some hidden wrong connected with her present position, and duty as well as inclination prompted me to search it out."

"Did you not say her eyes were blue," asked Katy.

"Blue as the summer sky."

"And her hair auburn ? "

"Ay, and beautiful as threads of gold."

"And her complexion fair ? "

"The lily is hardly fairer."

"Oh, she can only be my own 'Ginia. But then that Spanish name."

"There lies a mystery, she denies the name."

These questions were asked and answered, and Sinclair resumed his narrative : —

" I approach the sad catastrophe which resulted

in the death of my mother, and in my own captivity.

"With favoring winds, we had a short voyage,
and reached the mouth of the Ohio without accident. There we loaded, and remained a day for
the purpose of making some repairs upon the
barge. My mother and I walked out upon the
shore some distance to enjoy the cool shade of
some cottonwood trees, and we were fired upon by
Indians, within rifleshot of the barge and in sight
of Sister Naomi and Virginia. My poor mother
fell instantly dead, and I was captured and carried
off. I heard the screams of the women on the
boat as I was borne away to the woods.

"After being forced to travel on foot until
nearly exhausted, the savages placed me upon a
horse stolen from some settlement, and hastened
toward the prairies of the interior.

"The rest of my story you know. On the night
of the fourth day, your father and his noble band
rescued me from the savages ; and your family's
kindness since has nearly restored my usual
health."

CHAPTER VIII.

AN AMPHIBIOUS TOWN. — WORSHIP IN THE WOODS. —
"THE JERKS."

IT was widely known in "Illinois Territory," that
the goodly village of Shawneetown was subject
to frequent and unceremonious visits from *la belle
rivière*, and that this ordinarily genteel and well-
behaved stream was frequently known to come
when least expected, and to make a most ungentle
stay, notwithstanding the inhospitable reception it
met with from a people who are otherwise famed
for their hospitality. One of these unwelcome
overflows occurred about the time that Francis
Sinclair had sufficiently recovered from the effects
of his wound to begin to need and to desire out-
door exercise. His morning walks at first extended
far enough to enable him to take his breakfast with
a good appetite on his return ; but the flood having overflowed the land behind the town one night,
he was admonished to cut short his walk, or confine it to the river-bank, which was higher ground
than that behind the town.

On the next day the strip of dry land had narrowed to a quarter of a mile, and even that was fast disappearing. He began to feel somewhat uneasy, and on his return appealed to Katy Freeman to know what the people would do " if the river kept on rising."

" Well, my dear sir," said Katy pleasantly, " the river was never known to ' keep on rising.' "

" Oh, no," said Sinclair, " I trust it will stop some time. In the meantime, what will the people do ?"

" Oh, they will get into the upper part of the house, if the house happens to have an upper part. Others will caulk up their old boats, which have performed the same service on similar occasions before, and will move into them. Others will camp on those mounds which you observe above town : these are the last spots under water. Finally, when they can stay no longer, all go in the boats to the hills, and wait until the water goes down."

" Well," responded Sinclair, " that must be a delightful state of things ! I should prefer going to the hills before the flood comes — and never coming back. I judge from the movements of the people and the appearance of the water, which is still very muddy and filled with drift-wood, that there will have to be a general flight to the woods on this occasion."

"We have an opportunity," said Katy, "to go to the camp-meeting in the morning; and as it will continue for some time, the river will probably be down by the time of our return. Will you not be pleased to attend the meeting?"

"Indeed I will," he replied. "The scenes which I am told occur there are interesting to me on more accounts than one."

On the following morning Sinclair, accompanied by Mrs. Rose and party, got on board a small flat-boat, and started for the hills. As the party passed slowly on, Sinclair had a fine opportunity to observe the grotesque scene of a town under water. A few small artificial mounds, of aboriginal origin, and about three acres of dry ground at their base, was all of *terra firma* which could be seen. On those mounds, besides the cattle, horses, and dogs which had not been ferried to the hills, were men, women, and children, of all ages and colors, engaged in occupations as multifarious as their characters. Some were feeding stock, some were "killing their pork," some were gathering driftwood from the water, some were boiling tar for the purpose of pitching some old boat which had lain there idle since the last flood. Boats of all manner of shapes and sizes were passing to and fro between the mounds and the vacated houses. Flats, skiffs, canoes, rafts, and even horse-troughs, were put in requisition for this purpose ; one large flat-bottomed boat was doing service as a ferry-boat, carrying to the hills. A large portion of the population had already left the village, most of whom passed on to the camp-meeting on Cypress Creek, a few miles in the interior.

On reaching the camp-ground, Sinclair witnessed such a scene as could be found in no other country. The camp was located at a place most easily accessible to the people of all the "settlements" for many miles round; in the midst of a tall forest of oaks, hickories, pecans, and other towering trees. There were about forty tents or booths, built in a semi-circle round an open space of about three acres; and another circle, composed chiefly of covered wagons, surrounded this inner circle of tents. The tents were temporary huts of logs, and were intended chiefly as sleeping apartments. Between the circle of tents and the line of wagons large fires were burning ; at these the people prepared their food in the daytime, and they served to light the centre camp-ground at night. At a prominent central point the preachers' stand was erected. It consisted simply of a platform, four feet from the ground, built of slabs, supported by the same trees which served as the only covering above the heads of the preachers.

Our little party reached the camp-ground just after sundown. There were at least five hundred persons on the ground, gathered from a distance of thirty or forty miles around. Some of these were cooking their evening meal; some were singing hymns of praise in the various tents; while others were pouring out their hearts in fervent prayers.

Mrs. Rose had been invited by the Elder to occupy his tent in company with his own family, and thither the party proceeded. This Elder was a most devoted man of God. He had come all the way from Vincennes to attend this meeting; and he had labored so incessantly, preaching to the multitude, singing, praying, exhorting, and conversing with the people, that he was hoarse and nearly exhausted. But Elder Havens was not a man to give up. He had consecrated himself to the work, and was ready to fall in the battle with his harness on. Two or three other preachers also were at the meeting; and all labored with a zeal worthy of their cause.

After the frugal evening meal was disposed of, the people began silently to seat themselves on the rude benches in the open space in front of the preachers' stand, waiting in the most orderly manner for the services to begin. Occasionally some one would start an old familiar hymn, which would be caught up by the entire assembly, who made the very vault of heaven echo with their voices. Fresh fuel was put upon the fires, which threw their picturesque glare upon the tents, and cast a dim illumination over the whole assembly.

Presently the Elder rose, and in a solemn voice called upon the multitude to "unite in prayer." Oh, what a scene was that! The giant old trees of a thousand years spread their vast arms over the multitude, like the complex architecture of some huge Gothic temple; the blue sky vaulted it above, and the calm, bright stars looked down, like watchers in the spirit world. Then went up the voice of prayer to God from a temple the work of His hands. Then swayed the multitude of worshippers, as they were moved by the eloquence or the fervor of the preacher; and the deep amens, which ever and anon responded to his prayer, marked the deep devotion of the worshippers.

After the opening prayer a hymn was 'given out,' two lines at a time, and sung by the whole congregation with an earnest fervor which would put to shame the efforts of many of the more modern choirs.

After the preacher had announced the text, and had spent some time in elucidating it in his peculiar manner, Sinclair began to think, from the

stillness which prevailed, that he should not see
any of those scenes of excitement and physical
manifestation of which he had heard so much.
He had obtained a seat just in front of the preachers' stand, among the most devout of the brethren.
On the same seat with himself sat an old gentleman who had been introduced to him by the Elder
as Brother Sands.   There was something in the
appearance of this man which attracted Sinclair's
attention.   He was over six feet in height, very
slenderly made, and of a nervo-bilious tempera-
ment.   His body appeared to be almost without
bones in any part.   In the first place, his form
from head to foot was straight as an arrow.   His
legs and arms were not only marvellously straight,
but appeared to be without any increase in size
from his body outward.   His shoulders ran out
from his neck at a right angle, and the arms hung
down from them at a similar angle.   His hair was
straight and black, and his twinkling gray eyes
looked out from beneath straight, black brows, that
formed a line at right angles with his nose.   Even
his voice partook of this same angularity, never
passing from tone to tone by natural modulations,
but by a succession of inharmonious intervals.
This man was a devout Christian, whose life was
a worthy comment on his profession.

Some time after the sermon began, and before any undue excitement appeared in the congregation, the right arm of this man Sands suddenly flew up straight above his head, as if impelled by some unseen and irresistible force. The man gave a sudden, short, sharp shriek of pain. After a few seconds the arm fell as if dead to his side. In a moment more the other arm performed a similar movement and with increased violence. The man involuntarily cried out again with pain. Sinclair was alarmed, and took hold of the arm for the purpose of rendering some assistance. It was rigid as stone! The muscles on the top of the shoulders were thrown into a hard, knotty mass; and the whole limb felt as if it were made of wood instead of living flesh and blood. Some of the persons near requested Sinclair not to interfere in any way, as it would only make matters worse, adding that it was "nothing but the jerks." The arm soon fell down as the other had done; while the preacher, not at all interrupted by the occurrence, attended to his discourse as the more important duty.

After a little while the man's knees flew up into his face, and he fell to the ground perfectly helpless. Some of the brethren pulled him up and laid him upon some straw which had been spread

in front of the preachers' stand, where it had been
placed, in fact, for just such a purpose.   Here, the
man lay, suffering these contortions and "jerks,"
though less violent, until the close of the services.

Directly, a woman on the upper side of the
stand was attacked. Her jaws commenced jerking
with a short, quick bite, like the snapping of a
wolf.   The first paroxysm had caught her tongue
between her teeth, and had inflicted a wound
which was bleeding profusely.   She was placed on
the straw, also, to prevent injury from falling.
The contagion continued to spread until ten or
twelve persons had been drawn into the sympathetic circle, and lay helpless on the straw, jerking
more or less violently.

Then the character of the affection seemed to
be changed.   A woman suddenly fell from her
seat in a fit of convulsive laughter.   She was soon
followed by others, similarly affected, until more
than a dozen were engaged in this strange cachin-
ation.   This was chiefly confined to the women;
one poor creature laughed so incessantly that her
lungs became exhausted, and she presented the
appearance of a person dying from suffocation.
One of the preachers dashed a cup of cold water
in her face, when she caught her breath with a
sudden sigh, and resumed her respiration.

When the preacher had finished his discourse, he came down from the stand and passed round among the sufferers, addressing a few words of consolation to each one; and thus calmed the strange excitement he had raised. The arms and legs of Brother Sands, however, continued to perform their feats of triangulation for some time afterwards, and he was carried to his tent exhausted.

After the conclusion of the evening services, when all had retired to the tents for the night, Sinclair took occasion to converse with the Elder on the subject of the labors performed by the preachers of his denomination.

"I suppose, Mr. Havens," said he, "that such protracted efforts as are called for on this occasion are of comparatively rare occurrence?"

"Not at all, my dear sir," said the Elder. "I have attended four similar meetings in the course of the last four weeks, no two of which were within fifty miles of each other; and in no one of them have I had so much aid from other preachers as in this."

"Well," said Sinclair, "you will certainly be worn out after a while."

"Yes, thank God," said the Elder, "my Father will call me home in his own good time."

"Where is your permanent residence?"

"My wife and little ones are at Vincennes," said the Elder, "but my district extends over a hundred miles. Still, I manage to be with my wife and family five or six times a year."

"What remuneration do you receive?" inquired Sinclair.

"Remuneration? Oh, yes, God be praised!—a thousand times more than I deserve : the approbation of my Saviour,—'Well done, good and faithful servant!'"

"But your salary : you get some kind of support from the members, or you could not live?"

"Oh, yes; we all get a little something for food and raiment; but it is *so* little that no one is ever tempted to look upon *that* as his remuneration. I have a wife and five children; and I am allowed about two hundred and fifty dollars per annum. But I scarcely ever get over half that amount."

"But, my dear sir," said Sinclair, "it appears improbable that you could subsist at all on the whole amount, much less the half."

"It is truly a poor pittance," was the Elder's reply; "and nothing but the sustaining arm of a kind Providence enables us to bear up under it. For myself, I fare better than my poor wife and children; for I am visiting from church to church,

and always find some brother, who has more than
he needs for the present moment, to divide his
frugal meal with me, and then occasionally one
gives me a pair of shoes, or a hat, or even a coat;
so that I manage to get from one Conference to
another. But my poor family — without husband
and father, with none to watch over and protect —
theirs is a hard fate."

A tear stole into the corner of the good man's
eye as he continued : —

"I never murmur; and I only talk thus plainly
of a preacher's life in the West that you may be
able to realize the sacrifices which are made by
those who are carrying the Word of God into the
Wilderness. But I do not murmur. Many a time
and often, as I have been seated at the well-
provided table of some brother, a silent tear has
stolen down my cheek at the thought that my poor
wife and children were living on corn-bread and
water! Sometimes for many weeks not a mouth-
ful of any food was in my house but cornmeal; and
then we thanked God that this could be had so
cheap. A little salt and a little water and a little
fire, and the simple cornmeal becomes a wholesome
and pleasant bread. Let us thank God for Indian
corn! It has been the special friend of the Gospel
in this western country."

"I have seen the time, Brother Havens, when I could not get that," said another preacher who was present. "The year I was on the Wabash Circuit, our people paid their quarterage in corn. From that we fed our horses, cow, pigs, and chickens; and it was so far to the mill that we lived on hominy more than half the year, because we could not get our corn to the mill and back."

This last speaker was quite an old man; and Sinclair asked him how long he had been preaching.

"Thirty years," was the reply.

"Suppose you should die to-morrow: what would you be able to leave for the support of your family?"

"Not a penny!" said the other.

"Let us pray," said the Elder.

Then went up to God the fervent prayer of this man, who had consecrated his life, body and soul, to His service.

Sinclair retired to rest with new views of Christian duty; and a doubt, for the first time in his life, of the infallibility of the Romish Church.

The next day was the Sabbath; and the numbers in attendance had increased by several hundred, — consisting of hunters, boatmen, salt-boilers, negro slaves, etc., yet the most perfect good order prevailed throughout the day. At that time there were numbers of men who lived a life divided between hunting and agriculture. They raised a little corn, — or their wives did for them frequently, — just to feed themselves and their own stock, and perhaps a little for market; but still depended on the rifle as their chief means of support. These men and their rifles had become such inseparable companions that they were nearly always seen together. At home or abroad, in the field at work, in the village "tradin'," and even at " meeting," the rifle was always at hand.

About the camp-meeting, rifles might be seen here and there above the heads of the congregation. The men who carried them were, generally, in hunting attire; at one side of their girdles, by way of balancing the powder-horn at the other, there was generally seen a long-bladed hunting-knife, which would answer just as well for slashing "Injins" as wolves.

For the purpose of learning their character, Sinclair introduced to some of them the subject of the vote proposed to be taken throughout the Territory upon the question of the second form of government common to territories of that day.

"You backwoodsmen will have to lay by the rifle, and stick closer to the plough, after a while," said Sinclair.

"The territory will now make such an advance that a few years more will make it a State. It will hardly be forty years until there will be a million of people in it."

"Stranger," said a hunter named Edwards, formerly from Tennessee, "it is my opinion it is bad business, — this thing of crowding all the good land with people. The game is gettin' sca'ce a'ready."

"Yes, that may be," replied Sinclair, "but one plough will procure more of the necessaries of life than twenty rifles."

"Me and my boys can get all the necessaries for my family with our rifles. So can any man, as is a man. Howsomever — the women are gittin' to think a straw bonnet isn't good enough for 'em now; the boys have a Sunday coat; and the gals is all gittin' above wearin' linsey any longer."

"Yes, probably that is true," said Sinclair. "But many good things come with the increase of population which you cannot have without. You will soon have school-houses, and perhaps colleges after a while."

"Yes, stranger, that's the very thing. Let 'em git a skull-house, an' its *good-bye, spinnin' wheel !* No more ho'made jeans; nothin' but books an' romancin'."

"Are you opposed to books?" Sinclair ventured to inquire.

"In course I ain't," said the man. "I don't say that, but — I can put a ball through the centre, sixty yards, ten times, to any Yankee skule-master's once. They don't know a b'ar from a bugaboo."

"Still, my dear sir, the country would make poor progress without schools."

"Yes, that may all be true, stranger, as you say; but what's the use of progress? there's 'Squire Jones' family: I hain't nothin' agin 'em, but they believe in progress, — skules, 'cademics, and all that. Their gal Jane lets her mother work like a nigger, week in and week out, so as she may look nice and keep her hands soft, — that's progress. And that same gal turns up her nose at a youngster because he wears a hunting-shirt, — that's progress. I knew Jones the first time he ever seen broadcloth in his life: now look at him!"

"Still, I am told Mr. Jones is a very good man," said Sinclair.

"Oh, yes; Jones is a good enough fellow. He used to put a ball in a tin cup at a hundred yards; but progress spiled Jones as well as his gal. He sent that gal Jane to Vincennes, to the 'cademy there, and paid twenty dollars to have her learn to make music on a gatarr."

"To be able to play the guitar," said Sinclair, "is a very pretty accomplishment."

"It don't accomplish nothin' with her, but make a fool of the gal. She would rather *tum, tum, tum* on her banjo than help her poor old mother about the house."

Sinclair gave up the argument, satisfied that he had found a genuine frontiersman who would retreat before nothing but sunrise and civilization.

On the next morning the meeting was brought to a close. The preacher on "the Shawneetown Circuit," who resided for the present at a settlement half way between Shawneetown and another on the Wabash, thirty miles off, invited Sinclair, Mrs. Rose, and Katy to go with him and to remain for a few days, until the water should abate at Shawneetown. The invitation was accepted, and a ride of ten miles brought them to the humble home of Rev. Wesley Hobart.

CHAPTER IX.

THE residence of Mr. Hobart was a small, log-built house, with a loft above, in which a part of the family had their beds. It was situated on the brow of an eminence, on the outskirts of a heavy forest, and overlooking a beautiful plain in front. The plain, — a small prairie of a hundred acres or less, was bounded in the distance, on the northeast, by the Little Wabash River, a romantic stream, which gathers its waters up in the southern border of the great prairies, and among the forest trees between these and the true Wabash, and discharges them into that stream a short distance above its confluence with the Ohio, and it ran merrily along on that day as if nothing but health and happiness were to be found on its borders. From that little log-house on the hill, — the frontier parsonage, — the stream could be seen running off to the eastward, and disappearing in a distant forest of tall cypress trees. The little prairie in front of the parsonage was dotted with ten or fifteen log-houses, most of them but one story high, and consisting of a single apartment. The high ground on which the parsonage stood continued back in a southwest direction for many miles, covered with a tall forest, and broken into numerous hills and valleys. As the party who accompanied the preacher home approached the little settlement, and had pointed out to them the parsonage on the hill, they were impressed with the romantic beauty of the place. It was at that lovely season when the expiring year in that region assumes a thousand hues of beauty. The oaks, whose tall tops shaded the little house upon the hill, had doffed their deep-green hue and put on a livery of scarlet shaded deeply with brown. The maples had shed much of their foliage at the first frost, and the yellow leaves were carpeting the ground around their trunks. The sumach shone out in a suit of mottled scarlet and gold, and the whole forest was rich in the variegated tints of early autumn. Wild grapes were hanging in clusters from the trailing vines ; and a soft, balmy odor filled the breezes which came from the forest hills. It was one of those calm and gentle days in the Indian summer, when a hazy dimness pervades the atmosphere, and all nature seems to be resting in beauty.

"If I should give an opinion of the delightful

spot," said Sinclair to the preacher just before the party entered the house, "I should say it must be the very abode of health."

"You will find how nearly you have guessed," was the preacher's reply. "There is the doctor coming up to the house now. I fear that some of my family are sick."

They waited a moment for the doctor to come up. He was introduced as Doctor Hains; and all entered the preacher's door together. Mr. Hobart addressed his wife hastily, and as he extended his hand asked anxiously who was sick.

"Oh, no one," said the wife encouragingly. "Elizabeth and Sarah have the ague : that's all."

"That is *all!*" responded the preacher, looking toward Sinclair with a sorry smile. He then introduced his companion as a young gentleman from New Orleans, a friend of Mr. Rose's family, with whom she was already acquainted.

"What think you of your judgment now, friend Sinclair? Here are two subjects for the doctor under one roof," said the preacher.

"Rather an unpropitious beginning, I admit," replied Sinclair; "but I trust this is something unusual."

"It *is* rather unusual for my family to have but two cases of ague at once," responded Mr. Hobart.

"Well," said Sinclair, "down on that beautiful plain, — how is it there?"

"How is it, Doctor?" asked Hobart, well knowing what the reply would be.

"Much worse than up here," said the doctor. "There is less ague at this house every year than at any other in the settlement."

A pale, feeble girl now came down the rude ladder from the loft above. She was shaking violently with ague, and her jaws rattled involuntarily together.

"Elizabeth, my daughter," said the father, as he printed a kiss on her cold cheek, "I am sorry to see your chill back again."

The girl took a seat by the fire, where the mother was preparing the evening meal, and approached so near in the vain effort to warm her shivering limbs, that it appeared as if the skin must have been burned from her hands. She was about fifteen years old, naturally of slight frame, reduced by the ague almost to a skeleton. Her jet black eyes were rendered yet darker in appearance by the pallor of her skin; and her hair, from the same contrast, appeared of an inky blackness. Notwithstanding her suffering from fever and ague for months, there were still lingering traits of beauty about her, which impressed Sinclair as indicating greater culture than he expected to find in so wild a country.

The doctor examined the patient, left medicine for her; and then walking alone up the ladder to the loft above, as much at home as if in his own family, he there examined the other patient, left medicine with directions for its use, and returned to the room below.

"How is my little Sarah, Doctor?" asked Mr. Hobart.

"Sally's chill was pretty hard, but came on an hour later to-day than yesterday. She will hardly have more than two or three more," was the reply.

"Did you leave medicine?" inquired Mr. Hobart.

"I left 'barks' enough for ten days," replied the doctor. "I am going twenty-five miles to the Mc-Lean settlement to-morrow, and shall not be back till next day. Mr. Sinclair, I should be pleased to spend some time with you; but you will excuse me,—I have quite a number to see to-night. Good-bye, sir. Good-bye all."

And Doctor Hains started on his mission,—a mission which in a new country requires as much self-sacrifice as that of the Christian ministers.

Mrs. Hobart busied herself with the preparation of supper. The poor girl was still shaking with ague, and Sinclair began to feel a great interest in this disease, which appeared to have a victim in every family.

"The burden of doctors' bills must be considerable," said he; "and I should think, Mr. Hobart, that the doctor was quite certain to accumulate wealth."

"We preachers are at least exempt from that," said Mr. Hobart; "though it does appear as if we had more than our fair share of disease to struggle with."

"And how do you avoid doctors' bills?"

"No doctor would think of charging a minister," replied Mr. Hobart. "I never knew one to do so in the West; and in fact if one should do so he would soon have to leave the settlement. My family have taken nearly five pounds of Peruvian barks in the last year, — worth a dollar a pound, — all furnished by the good Doctor Hains; and if I should ask him for his bill he would be offended. As to the doctors getting rich, I think you are mistaken there also. The people are too poor and have too much sickness to be able to pay much in the way of doctors' bills. No, no; doctors get rich only among a rich people; and those are to be found in the healthful regions, not the sickly ones."

"*Five pounds of barks*, did you say?"

"Yes," replied the preacher. "I think we have used fully five pounds during the year."

"Why, my dear sir, this is horrible! And will nothing do but the eternal bark, bark, bark? How many have you in your family?"

"We have one son and two daughters: it's just a pound apiece."

By this time the "chill" had nearly passed off the daughter, who sat by the fire; and as the fever began to rise, she left the fireplace and took a seat near the door to obtain the benefit of the cool evening air. She now joined in the conversation.

"I have taken a pound and a quarter myself, Mr. Sinclair," she said. "How much more I shall need I cannot guess."

"Do you have ague *all* the time?" inquired Sinclair.

"Oh, no, sir," said she; "not more than half the time. It is beginning to wear out, too. I do not have it so bad as formerly."

"Ah, my daughter," said the preacher in a tone of sadness, "it is *you* are wearing out; and, unlike the terrible disease, passing away never to return."

The girl came and sat upon his knee and threw her arms about his neck.

"Don't talk so sadly, my dear father," said she. "The doctor says I shall be more healthy than ever when I get well."

"Still living on hope, Elizabeth!" said the father. "Bless God for hope! It has borne us up, Mr. Sinclair, when all but God was gone."

Just now the other daughter came down from the loft, and hastened with a kiss to her father's side. She was twelve years old, of fair complexion, and with light hair and blue eyes, like her mother.

"And here is my blue-eyed girl with cheeks redder than ever with the flush of fever. How do you feel, Sarah?" said the father.

"My head is still aching, father," said the girl, in a voice of silvery tone, which instantly reminded Sinclair of the lost Virginia. "But," the child added, "my chill was very slight."

During this conversation, Mrs. Hobart had been silently getting ready the supper; and having arranged her table for her guests, she now came forward and invited them to partake.

Mrs. Hobart was a lady of education and refinement. She was the daughter of a wealthy gentleman living near Lexington, in Kentucky, who had discarded her because she persisted in being a Methodist.

Sixteen years before she had been married to Mr. Hobart, and had given up the life of ease and luxury in which she had grown up, to share the toils and trials of a preacher's life in the wilderness. She had possessed very considerable personal beauty, before time and the trials of a frontier life had made their ravages; and even yet, though she was beyond the meridian of life, her blue eyes were as radiant with the light of the soul within as in her palmy days of youth. She was a woman of great fortitude, exhibiting that admirable combination of gentleness and courage, of susceptibility and great power of endurance, — which so frequently strikes us as incompatible, and makes us wonder how such apparently opposite traits can be mingled in the same character. There was really no incompatibility about her, however. The mere mortal was feeble, shrinking from every touch of injury or evil; but the immortal defied all the ills of the present, and looked with undimmed hope to a better future. And this ever-trusting, never-dying hope had sustained her, and enabled her to console her despairing husband when he would otherwise have fallen by the wayside of life.

The evening meal, of which she now called on her guests to partake, was spread upon a cloth of domestic linen white as driven snow; the simple fare had been prepared by her own delicate hands, and everything had that air of exquisite neatness which gives such an inviting charm to the plainest food.

The bread was made of Indian meal, but the modest little "dodgers" were baked precisely to that exquisite tint of golden brown, so difficult to attain, and so necessary to the finest flavor. The tea, to be sure, was not the product of the Celestial Empire ; but its rich, amber-colored stream, as it poured from the steaming urn, sent an aroma through the apartment which placed the Western sassafras on a par with its Oriental rival. The sugar had never been submitted to the refining influence of bullock's blood and gum, but had been prepared from the maple-tree by her own hands. The hominy was white as snow, and the plump grains, instead of being boiled to a pulp and spoiled, lay in the white dish distinct as hailstones ; while the delicately cut slices of dried venison lay so lightly on the green-edged plate that the rosy light played through them most invitingly.

The whole party did ample justice to the supper, not excepting the two daughters, whose cheeks still wore the flush of intermittent fever.

"I am pleased to see that your daughters have an appetite," remarked Sinclair, "and hope it bodes an early recovery."

"Ah, my dear sir," said Mr. Hobart, "that is one of the subterfuges of this fell demon!—for there seems to be a very demon about it, — first shaking the breath from its victims, then calling upon them to eat and recover strength for another ordeal. I believe none of its promises."

Mrs. Hobart replied to her husband's remarks with a smile.

"You see, Mrs. Rose," said she, "my husband still looks on the shady side."

"Yes," replied Mrs. Rose; "that's his way, I suppose."

"Life has but two sides," said the preacher. "The shady side is mortality, the bright one is eternity. Did we not look beyond this life to a better, gloomy indeed would be our existence."

"Still, Wesley," said the wife, "why should we seek out all the gloomier paths to the better world, and neglect all the flowers which a kind Providence strews by the wayside?"

"Yes, yes; I know," said the preacher. "Were the world filled with such as my own dear wife, we should forget our destiny."

The preacher spoke in such a tone of sadness that his guests were touched by the same feeling, and but little more was said to the close of the meal. While the reader imagines the wife removing the dishes from the table, he may as well gain a better insight into the character of her very kind but very despondent husband, the preacher.

Wesley Hobart was forty years old, of fair proportions, and of an industrious though sluggish disposition. His complexion was dark and his hair and eyes strikingly black. Although of untiring perseverance, his thoughts and movements were slow, and all he did deliberate. He added to a great firmness of purpose and perseverance in action, a distrust of the future and a tendency to despond, which required the constant aid of his religious sentiments to bear him up. He was a native of Virginia, a preacher of religion in early life, and had joined the Methodists at a time when they were in some degree a despised sect. Shortly afterward he was impelled from a strong sense of duty to migrate to Kentucky for the purpose of preaching the gospel. At Lexington he saw and married his wife, with a warning from her father that he would disown and disinherit his daughter. He found a kind and dutiful wife, and he loved her most devotedly ; but the trials he had brought upon her by introducing her to the life of a preacher on the frontier had been to him ever since a constant source of annoyance and sorrow. The wife herself was always hopeful, and never murmured; but this only added to his regret. His ability as a preacher was but moderate, but his labors of love among his people more than compensated for any deficiency in rhetoric or oratory. For fifteen years he had never failed to attend the annual Conferences of his church, though frequently compelled to go great distances to reach them, and under the most discouraging circumstances. During the last eighteen months he had been suffering frequent attacks of ague and fever. He had bravely struggled on, however, and preached at all his regular appointments, sometimes in the midst of the chill or the succeeding fever. He was a devoted minister, a kind husband and father, and was universally esteemed for his consistent piety. Such was Wesley Hobart.

When supper was over, and the preacher with his family and guests were seated together, Mrs. Rose and Katy both inquired for Joseph, the preacher's son, who had not made his appearance since his father's return.

"Joseph went to town this morning," said the mother, "to see if there were letters for us at the post-office."

"Do you send all the way to Shawneetown?" inquired Katy.

"Oh, yes," replied Mrs. Hobart, "there is no

other way, that is the nearest post-office. Fourteen miles is a long way to send the little fellow; but he knows the road and has often gone before."

"How old is your son?" inquired Sinclair.

"Joseph is ten years old," replied the mother.

"Poor boy," said Mr. Hobart, "it is time he should be home. I fear something detains him."

"Why, what can detain him, dear?" said the mother.

"Well, the water may still be up, so that he has had to ferry from the hills."

"It is certainly a long distance to send for your letters," said Sinclair, "and for so small a lad to go too. Is it not already night?"

"The moon will shine," said Mrs. Hobart, "he will soon be here."

"Does he have the terrible ague too?" inquired Sinclair.

"Not for more than a month past," replied the mother.

"What a scourge it is!" remarked Sinclair.

The preacher heaved a deep sigh. He had been sorely tried by the disease in his family, and seldom let pass an opportunity to visit upon "the demon" (as he termed it) his malediction.

"Mr. Sinclair," said he, "we have suffered more by the demon than tongue can tell."

"Oh, no," said Mrs. Hobart. "We have suffered very much, truly; but I know a tongue which can tell all about it."

"But isn't it a sad, sad story?"

"Yes, it is both a sad one and a long one," said the wife; "but I never knew how much I loved my husband, my children, or my Saviour, till the ague came among us. I can trace the kind hand of Providence through it all. For three months, Mrs. Freeman, every soul in the family had the ague; but never in all that time were we all down at the same hour."

"Think of that, sir," said the preacher, but in a tone which did not partake of the same trustful hope as his wife's. "I preached from one appointment to another, suffering under its scourge, leaving my wife and three little ones at home all stricken by the same disease."

"Still, when a part were down, others would be up to wait on them; sometimes Elizabeth, Sarah, and I were all sick at once, but then Joseph's chill was sure to be off, and he waited on us all so tenderly. The dear boy would come to my bedside and ask, 'Mother, what shall I do for your poor head?' It appeared to do him good even to give us a drink of water. Sometimes all were down but Sarah, and the sweet child would try so hard 'to get mother

and sister a nice cup of tea,' as she would say.
The next day, perhaps, *she* would be down, and it
would be Elizabeth's turn to nurse. Lizzie is
always cheerful, and can almost charm away the
chill with her hopeful words. Oh, yes," she continued, " terrible as it is, the ague may be sanctified
to our hearts for good."

" *Your* heart, my dear wife," said the preacher,
" seems to throw a gleam of sunshine upon the
darkest passages of life. I fear, Mr. Sinclair, my
religion is only a partial one : it has never been
fully able to overcome the weakness of the flesh.
With my wife it is deep and thorough ; not only
does it enable her to look with the spirit's eye
through hope to a better world, but it seems to
soothe like a heavenly opiate all the ills of this
mortal frame."

" There comes brother !" exclaimed the sisters
simultaneously, as the sound of horses' hoofs was
heard approaching the door.

It had been many years, — years full of tribulation, — since Mrs. Hobart had received a letter
from her father, though she occasionally heard
from her kindred through the letters of a sister
still in Kentucky. When, therefore, Joseph handed
her a letter postmarked " Lexington," and she
recognized her father's well-known hand in the

superscription, she eagerly broke the seal to know if her father, — to whom she had always been devotedly attached, — had really so far relented as to write to his cast-off daughter. And when she discovered that such was the fact, and that he addressed her as his *dearest daughter*, the tears burst from her eyes, — tears which long and cruel neglect had never been able to wring from her, — and she asked her guest's indulgence while she retired to the loft above to read the long-hoped-for letter.

"Well, Joseph, my son," said the preacher, "you have had a tedious journey to-day."

"O father," replied the boy, not heeding his parent's words, "I saw the Pigeon Roost! There were millions and millions and *millions* of them. I have more of them on Old Gray at the door, than we can eat in a week."

Joseph had inherited his mother's disposition to find enjoyment in everything, and was not at all disposed to look on the shady side of life; he had seen the wild pigeons passing in innumerable hosts to their nightly roost, and the sight more than repaid him for his long ride to the post-office. As he passed the outskirts of the roost, the kind people had supplied him with as many of the plump, fat birds as he could carry. In answer to his

father's remark he hastened to the door, and returned with his trophies.   As the girls retired to
prepare some of them for breakfast on the coming
morning, Sinclair turned to the preacher and remarked : —

"I think, Mr. Hobart, that the disposition to be
happy or unhappy, sad or cheerful, is in a great
measure constitutional, and that it may descend
from parent to child.   All of your children, for
example, appear to inherit your good lady's disposition to view all things in the best light."

"I believe you are right," said the preacher,
"though it required many years' observation to
satisfy me of the fact.   It has been my sad priv-
ilege, Mr. Sinclair, to witness the death-scene of a
large number of persons, and the various manner
in which men pass from mortality to the hidden
world is a profound mystery, without some such
explanation.   There was old Mr. Hathaway, on the
river ; to me his death was absolutely terrible, but
he regarded it merely as a physical phenomenon of
little importance.   He was truly an unbeliever, if
ever there was such a man.   I tried by all the
means in my power to awaken within him a sense
of his condition, but all in vain.   When I told him
he was certainly dying, he answered, 'yes, the
frail old machine is almost worn out.'   'And yet,'

I would reply, " you have no hope of immortality.'
'Oh, yes,' he would reply, "I shall live on in my
children.'

"And that was *his* hope. The mortal form which
still held his immortal soul was to his mind a
machine; and he was immortal only in his offspring. And this man died calmly and peacefully.
May God have mercy on his soul."

The preacher's voice trembled with the deep
earnestness of his prayer.

"I knew a man," said Sinclair, "who, when told
that he was dying, turned to his wife and said,
'Well, Sally, the jig's up; it's no use crying.'
They were the last words he uttered."

Early next morning, after a hurried meal, Sinclair, Mrs. Rose, and Katy started on their return
to Shawneetown. Before following them, let us
return to the preacher and his family, and learn
the termination of a notable episode.

It is probable that the sorest trial which can
befall a sensitive mind is one which places all the
social feelings at variance with the religious sentiments, — the love of husband or wife and children,
and all that relates to their temporal welfare, on
the one hand, and the stern dictates of religious
duty on the other, opposing that welfare and demanding its sacrifice. Such was the conflict which

arose in the mind of Mrs. Hobart on reading the letter from her unrelenting father. When he cast her off for joining the Methodists, and setting his will at defiance by uniting her destiny with that of a preacher of the sect he despised, he had determined to cast her off absolutely and forever; and although for years his naturally ardent parental feelings had prompted him to relent, still he had maintained an unbroken silence toward her.

As he grew older, however, his parental feelings gained the ascendancy, and for years he had longed for an opportunity to reconcile his pride and his affection. His only other child, a daughter, still unmarried, was fast hurrying to a consumptive's grave; and he felt that his home would soon be left desolate. He knew through Mrs. Hobart's letters to her sister all the history of her privation and suffering, and especially of the consolation she had found in her kind and dutiful children. At length he could bear it no longer. His heart became fixed upon his grandson Joseph, and in a moment of strong emotion he wrote to his daughter, for the first time in years. It was this letter which Joseph had brought from the post-office at Shawneetown, and which Mrs. Hobart had retired to the loft to read.

The letter opened in the kindest manner, and as

if nothing had occurred to interrupt the relation naturally existing between them, invited the whole family to return to Lexington and enjoy her father's bounty, and referred to his grandchildren as his future heirs. After the signature at the bottom was the following postscript :—

"There will no longer be any necessity for your husband's preaching, and I of course shall expect him to give it up."

When Mrs. Hobart had opened the letter, her first sensation was one of surprise that her father had at last written to her in kindness. Then, as she read farther, her heart swelled with gratitude, and she was nearly overcome with emotion. Could it be possible that the long estrangement was over; that penury had done its work; and that she was about to see her dear children placed above the reach of want, and happy in the smiles of a grandfather whose heart she knew by her own early days was full of kindness, notwithstanding the cruel banishment which had fallen upon her own head? The thought almost rendered her delirious with gladness. While in this state of feeling her eye fell upon the postscript. She glanced at it; then, as if doubting her eyes, re-read it carefully word by word, and in an audible voice. The letter then fell from her hand, and her whole frame was seized with trembling. Large drops of sweat, cold and clammy, broke out upon her temples, and a sense of some impending and terrible danger took possession of her.

When she was sufficiently recovered to collect her scattered thoughts, she bowed herself in prayer, and supplicated the Heavenly Father whom she so devotedly worshipped to deliver her from temptation.

When Mr. Hobart ascended to the loft he found his wife suffering from the effects of her extreme agitation. To his anxious inquiries as to the cause of her trouble, she replied only by putting her father's letter into his hands. He read it through in silence; though he felt, if possible, even more deeply than did his wife, the sore temptation which was thrown in his way, not a sound escaped his lips. He knelt beside his wife and communed in silence with his Maker.

After a short time Mrs. Hobart rose, calmly held her father's letter in the flame of the candle, and after seeing it burn to ashes, said, " God is still with us. Let us retire." Not another word was spoken by either that night.

Next morning, when the preacher came down to breakfast, he found his wife moving about her household duties with an expression of countenance which appeared almost angelic. Not a trace of sorrow, not the least lingering mark of the struggle through which she had passed on the night before, was to be seen. She spoke to her children in tones of cheerfulness which startled her husband from the intensity of their calmness.

Hobart seated himself at the table and attempted to eat. But the thought of the terrible sacrifice which that delicate and feeble woman had voluntarily made for him and for the Gospel's sake made him almost loathe his food. His thoughts wandered back over the long years of tribulation she had borne without a murmur; the loneliness, the privation and sickness, the loss of home, father, and friends, and the whole train of temporal ills which had befallen her since her lot had been cast with his. He thought of what she had renounced, — the prospect of instant and complete relief held out by her father's letter, — ease and luxury, friends and home for her children; and all for him, a poor, unworthy Methodist preacher! It was too much; and the poor, shattered form was unable longer to bear the struggles of the agitated soul within. He left the table; reached a chair; and immediately vomited a large quantity of blood, almost suffocating from its profusion. It lasted only a minute, but so exhausted him that he was with difficulty able to make his way to the bed.

The doctor was immediately sent for, and the breakfast hurried away untasted.

The preacher beckoned his wife to his bedside, and taking her hand in his said, with a peculiar light in his countenance, —

"My Father calls. I am going home."

"O my dear husband," said the wife, "I hope you will soon be better."

"Yes, dear wife," said he, — "a few hours, at most, and no ill can ever reach me more. Blessed be God! Though His providence may be inscrutable, it is always just and good."

He was interrupted by another hemorrhage. The doctor came in; and seeing that the blood was very dark, and not of the bright red he had expected, told the preacher he had hopes of his recovery.

"You are very kind, Doctor," said the sufferer; "but my hour is come. All remedy will be unavailing." Then, addressing his wife, he continued: "It was all a terrible mystery how a just God could visit *you* with affliction for my sake. Oh, it's all plain now. You have passed the fiery ordeal in triumph, and now God is going to take me to Himself, and thus send you and our little ones to the abundance and protection of your father's home."

Seeing his wife in tears, he said, "Not a tear,— not a tear. It could not at most have been many years before my labors here would end, and then I might have suffered the pangs of some dreadful disease; but now I have not a pain, — not a single pain."

Attacks of hemoptysis continued to occur, and he rapidly lost strength, and finally consciousness. Before this occurred he had called his children around him and taken an affectionate leave of them, telling them to be prepared to follow him to that heavenly mansion to which he was going.

An hour or two before his death, his wife observed that his sight seemed to be failing him. She took his hand and said, —

"Your sight is dim; your eyes are failing, my husband."

"Oh, no," he replied; "they are only looking inward and upward. Oh, the ecstatic vision which breaks upon my view!"

His utterance was interrupted by the spouting blood, and he spoke no more. But a calm composure rested on his countenance; and pressing his wife's hand to the last, he died without a struggle. The wheel was broken at the cistern, the pitcher was broken at the fountain, and the preacher was done with toil.

A few days after the death of her husband, Mrs. Hobart disposed of the few household goods of any value which she possessed; and with her children commenced her sad journey to her father's house.

CHAPTER X.

GOING from the house of Mr. Hobart to
Shawneetown, the route of Sinclair and his
friends lay along the Indian path at the foot of the
range of hills which borders the wide "bottom"
extending for some distance up the Wabash to the
town, where it sweeps away to the Saline River,
ten miles lower down the Ohio. The waters had
so far subsided as to offer little obstruction to
their progress; but their way was obstructed here
and there by large piles of drift-wood left by the
receding river. When they reached the town,
some time after noon, they found it still separated
from the hills by running water; but the water
was not deep, and with the boldness of dwellers
on the frontier, Mrs. Rose and Katy urged their
horses into the stream, telling Sinclair that they
knew where the road lay, and calling upon him to
follow.

The village offered a curious spectacle. Almost

the whole population was engaged in scrubbing out the houses. The river had left a sediment of clay and sand upon the floors; and the people were doing their best to make the same stream act as chief agent in removing it. Mops and brooms were dashing the now receding waters upon the muddy floors; and a ready joke or a merry laugh could be heard at almost every door.

When the party arrived at home old Tabby met them, with her shining face, boasting of her exploits.

"Tank fortin', Missus," said Tabby, "you's gwine into de cleanes' house in de Territory. I scrub out de house de fus' one in town; dey doesn't git ahead o' old Tabby, if she am old."

This was followed by a chuckle of self-satisfaction, and a throwing open of doors to let in the light, and enable her mistress to see how well she had performed her duty.

"Dey aint gwine to git ahead o' old Tabby!" she again exclaimed. Had any one else called her *old* Tabby, she would have been mortally offended. She claimed the right to the cognomen of "Aunt Tabby," though so far as any one knew she had neither niece nor nephew in the world.

"It does young massa good to go to de camp meetin'", the old woman continued, as the party entered and seated themselves in the house. "He was mighty good lookin' befo' de doctor bore de hole in his head, an' bin gittin' better lookin' eber sence." Having delivered herself of this compliment, she retired to the kitchen to prepare an early supper, or late dinner.

It may be that the reader would like to have such a description as would enable him to form an opinion as to the correctness of Aunt Tabby's judgment, when she pronounced the young man "good lookin'."

Admitting that the appearance of the outward man is of little consequence compared with the immortal within, yet it is universal custom when we are learning the attributes of a character, to clothe it also, in the mind's eye, with form ; and, to make possible a clear conception of the individual, the portrayal must be correct and careful. For say what we will on the subject, there is a harmony between form and character, which, although difficult to describe, may be very easily seen and appreciated. Suppose, for example, that Mr. Sinclair should be described as having red hair, a white and diaphanous complexion, and a soft, inelastic skin ; the observant reader perceives that though such a man might possibly fall in love with a blue-eyed girl of thirteen, during a three-months' voyage up

the Mississippi, his love would not be at all likely
to survive a week's captivity with the Indians, and
the boring of an inch hole in his cranium.

Be good enough now to imagine Mr. Francis
Sinclair as a young gentleman with very dark
chestnut hair, a fair complexion tending to a brown,
and a skin of delicate and elastic texture, which,
instead of resembling wet parchment, gave every
indication of being endowed with life. Let his
eyes be blue, so very blue as to be generally mistaken for black; his height five feet eight, or possibly ten inches; his flesh firm, with a round de-
velopment of the muscles; his carriage upright,
and his step firm and decided. These were the
more obvious features and characteristics of the
man. But such an observer as the Swiss philosopher Lavater might have noticed the indications
of great firmness in the drawing down of the angles
of the mouth, and of great kindness in the elevation of the same angles; of defiant sternness in
the depression of the inner angles of the eye-
brows, and of quick humor in the elevation of
the outer ones. But the deductions to be drawn
from so careful an analysis, though they may reach
the truth, are yet too critical for the ordinary
observer. It is well enough to know, however,
that Mrs. Katy Freeman approved the judgment

of Aunt Tabby. And she thought, whatever might be the lot of her lost 'Ginia, she must have passed some pleasant hours with her *compagnon de voyage* up the Mississippi River.

The morning after his return to Shawneetown, Sinclair found letters at the post-office from his uncle at St. Louis, containing remittances of money, which he much needed; and also replies to inquiries he had made, in a letter written to his uncle soon after recovering from the effects of his wound, as to the presence of Sister Naomi and her young charge at St. Louis. The uncle wrote that they had left his boat at St. Genevieve; and that he had not been able to learn anything of them since. Sinclair communicated this intelligence to Mrs. Freeman, and told her that he had resolved to visit St. Louis at the first opportunity; and if her daughter was not to be found there, then he would go to St. Genevieve, and, if possible, trace her out from thence. Tim Rose had not yet returned from New Orleans, where he had gone to search for 'Ginia; but as Sinclair felt assured she was not in that city, he would not await her uncle's return.

During the day Sinclair had an opportunity of witnessing the migration of the wild pigeons, which were passing over the river from Kentucky

to the woods, ten miles northeast of the town.
They began to pass over the town about three
o'clock in the afternoon, and were still passing in
innumerable hosts when darkness shut them from
view.   The sight was new to Sinclair, and so full
of wonder that he gave himself up to the observation for several hours.

First the birds came in sections of a few hundreds together ; then in large numbers, — platoons,
companies, regiments, brigades, — and then like
an army in solid column.   And so, like a living
stream, they poured along for two hours or more.
Afterwards smaller divisions, more and more
broken into groups, came on until darkness hid
them from view.   One thing struck Sinclair with
peculiar surprise : the line of flight had in it
occasional curves, and to those curves the whole
vast multitude conformed.   When the advance
sections were first seen crossing the river above
the town, they performed the passage in a double
curve, — heading downward almost to the surface
of the river and rising again without touching it ;
and afterward the whole multitude followed the
same line with critical exactitude.   For the first
time in his life Sinclair was disposed to doubt the
evidence of his eyes, and even of his ears ; for the
sound made by the flapping of innumerable wings

was like "a rushing mighty wind." The main army of birds was about half a mile in breadth, — the birds flying closely together as their wings would permit, — and the living stream unbroken for hours!

Finding that a number of persons were going to visit the roost next day, he determined to make one of the party, and see the wonder for himself. The company consisted of Mr. Wilson, the landlord, Tom Summers, Lynch, and a young lawyer named Calvard. This man Calvard was a fair type of a class of men, then and still common in the West, who have exerted a great influence on its destiny. He was a native of Ohio; and although only about twenty-five years old had made as much advance in a knowledge of the world as most men have made at fifty. He was a bold, fearless thinker on all subjects, a native orator, and an uncompromising Democrat.

The distance to the outskirts of the roost was about ten miles; and as the party rode leisurely along in their wagon they improved the time by the interchange of thought and opinion; and as all the party with the exception, perhaps, of Mr. Wilson and Sinclair, were remarkable for an inclination to "wreak their thought upon expression," Sinclair had ample opportunity to inform himself

on the subjects of backwoods philosophy and
frontier politics before they reached the pigeon
roost.

Mr. Wilson possessed a happy faculty of drawing
out the thoughts of others, while he kept his own
in reserve, or perhaps indicated them by the character of his interrogations.

"Gentlemen," said Mr. Wilson, addressing the
party generally, "where under heaven do you
suppose such a raft of pigeons came from ?"

"My opinion, squire," said Lynch, "is that they
are just hatched, like other birds."

"Yes; but, Lynch, there's fifty thousand wagon
loads of them at this one roost. Suppose we add
all the roosts together; there will be more pigeons
than all the other birds in the world."

"So there ought to be," said Summers, taking
up the answer, "if they are like tame pigeons.
They hatch a nest full ten or twelve times every
year."

"Don't you know," interposed Mr. Calvard,
"that there is never more than one roost at the
same time ? Last year it was near Dayton, in
Ohio; year before, in Kentucky; now it is here.
Everything," he continued with an air of conviction, "indicates that it is so. In the first place,
there is never known to be more than one roost in

the same year. In the second place, it is known that the pigeons of a single roost will gather and consume the food in a circuit of a thousand miles round. A gentleman in Kentucky told me they consumed every acorn in the Oak Flats, — which cover twenty miles square, — in two days. In the third place, the numbers are so vast, that more than two or three such roosts as this would consume all the food on the continent in a short time, and then perish of starvation. I think there is little doubt that all the pigeons in the world, except stragglers, gather in one roost, and that their rapid flight enables them to feed over so vast an extent of country, that they are thus able to find their sustenance."

" Do you find that in your books, Calvard?" inquired Summers.

"Books? No!" replied he, with a sneer. "The book of the backwoods is not yet written, on any subject. Where is the book of backwoods politics, or philosophy, or religion? I tell you that this Valley of the Mississippi will yet teach the world a new lesson on all these subjects."

"I'm afraid," said Tom, "there won't be any backwoods after a while, as things is agoing."

"No matter for the woods," replied Calvard. "The same bold, self-reliant, and independent peo-

ple will still be here ; the same cheap food, cheap
raiment, and well-paid labor ; the same stimulating
and invigorating climate, and the same bright and
cheerful skies : these all produce their effects on
the character of the people.   Then, thank God !
we have no veneration for old usages and old cus-
toms as such ; we have no respect for precedents,
only as they may happen to be right, and of that
we judge for ourselves.

"Then we have no aristocratic university," he
continued, "to sanction a false philosophy, or
established church to sustain a false religion.   We
have what the world never saw before, Mr. Wilson, — a people with strong, cultivated minds, untrammelled by hoary errors, and hence, free to
investigate truth in politics, morals, and religion,
as has never yet been done."

Tom Summers listened to these expressions with
profound attention.

"Calvard," said he, "how did you ever happen
to be a lawyer ? you don't learn this from the law
books, — old Blackstone and the like ?"

"If Blackstone had been an Illinois farmer,"
replied Calvard, "he would have written about as I
talk.   He brought all the order possible out of the
confusion he found in England : here there is no
confusion, no old errors nor established wrongs ;

and he would have been free to develop the Law of Right. There he commented on the law of England ; here he would only point out the natural law which grows out of the relations of man to man when they stand as equals."

" What do you think of these smoke-boats ? " said Tom. " They will drive all the boatmen out of the country. That ain't justice ; it can't be right."

" Yes, it will be," replied Calvard, "and when they have employed you at good wages for twenty years, you will be ready to acknowledge it is all right. The steamboats must have pilots ; and none are so good as the old keel-boatmen. No, no, Tom ; the steamboats will enable us to build an empire in fifty years, such as the world never saw ; and it will be an empire in which you and I and all of us will be emperors."

" Whoop ! " exclaimed Tom, with a yell of delight at the anticipation of realizing hopes which, although they had floated vaguely in his own mind for years, now first found form in these words from the lips of Calvard, " whoop, hurra ! we've got the largest rivers, the deepest lakes, the biggest mountains, and the greatest country in the world."

" Hurrah for old Kaintuck ! " exclaimed Lynch, catching the spirit of Tom's patriotism. " Kaintuck is jist in the centre of the airth."

" How much farther do we go," inquired Sinclair,
" before we reach the pigeon roost ? "

" Look thar ! " responded Lynch.   " That's the
way they do it."

He pointed to a large chinquapin oak by the
roadside, stripped of its leaves, and its branches
torn and broken from the weight of the birds upon
them the night before.

" Can it be possible," inquired Sinclair, " that
this is really the work of birds ? "

" Even so," said Mr. Wilson.

The party now reached the borders of the forest
in which the pigeons had established their roost ;
and they soon began to meet persons loaded down
with the game.   A mile or two farther on they
halted for the night in the midst of a heavy forest.
They pitched their tent near a spring of pure
water, and in the vicinity of other tents put up by
parties who had preceded them, some of whom had
been there several days, and were now engaged in
" jerking " the birds obtained the night before.
Vast piles of dead pigeons were lying around, and
men, women, and children were preparing them for
carrying away.   This was done by taking the
breasts alone, stringing them on sticks, and drying
them rapidly before fires which were kept constantly burning.   Some of the men had become so

expert that they would separate the breast from the bird by a peculiar twist of the hands, and so rapidly that one man could "strip" the breasts from the birds as fast as three or four could string them and get them before the fire. The rejected portions were thrown to the hogs, which had been driven in for the purpose of consuming them. The roost extended over several miles, and on all sides were collected persons who came to assist in the havoc, and to jerk and carry off the game.

About the middle of the afternoon, the birds began to arrive, — first in small parties, and disposed to avoid the vicinity of the tents, — then in large bodies, consisting of hundreds of thousands, and paying little attention to the presence of man ; and at last they came in such immense numbers that the sky was obscured. Their wings made a noise like that of a hurricane, and they alighted upon the trees in such masses as to break off huge limbs, which came crashing down, killing large numbers of birds in their fall. As night came on the birds which came latest, finding all places occupied, and "no rest for the soles of their feet," attempted to perch upon trees already full, till the overloaded branches would fall bringing all down together. The people aided in the havoc, attacking the falling masses of birds with sticks and clubs, so that long before midnight there were more dead birds than could be disposed of all next day.

But though man, their enemy, had from sheer satiety ceased from slaughter, the cracking and falling of branches and the dropping of the wounded birds continued until morning. Then came the excitement of the departure. Before it was fully daylight the advance squadrons were in motion, their wings making a noise like a tornado, and filling the air with leaves and small branches torn from the trees. Before sunrise all that could fly were off south for Kentucky, and those which could not fly fell victims to man and to that inevitable accompaniment of civilization, the hog.

The whole scene was so exciting that Sinclair looked on in silence for hours. At length, when the living tide had ebbed back to the mountains of Kentucky, he turned to Calvard, —

"I give up, I am beaten, — I am convinced," he said. "Yesterday I laughed at your theory that all the pigeons in the world are congregated at the same roost. To-day I adopt it as the only one which is at all plausible."

"I believe it," replied Calvard; "it agrees with all the facts. In fact, Mr. Sinclair, this is the country in which to study to advantage the character of a creature much higher in the scale of being than a wild pigeon. What do the philosophers of Europe know of man's character and capabilities? They study him crowded, hampered in cities, hungry, half naked and half sick; they observe him under the restraint of partial laws, hereditary privileges, and restricted energies; and they must almost necessarily mistake his true character. Here all there is in him will come out and manifest itself, and he may be studied under the most favorable circumstances. And here, therefore, all honest men have admitted his capacity to govern himself."

While the party were loading their wagon with game, Mr. Wilson continued the conversation by inquiring of Calvard whether he thought the experiment of man's self-government had yet been fairly tested.

"No, sir," replied Calvard; "it never will be fairly tested until universal suffrage is established. Let every man vote for every officer, and by himself or his representative have a voice in every law: then it will be fairly tried."

"That's it, 'Squire," said Tom Summers. "I'm for that, and all of it."

"Would you elect judges by the people?" inquired Mr. Wilson.

"Yes, everything," replied Calvard. "The people, as a rule, will always choose the best men."

Mr. Wilson shook his head. He felt that the experiment would be a dangerous one, and he was too cautious a man to be willing to risk much in experiment. But Calvard, now fairly started on his favorite topics, defended his views on universal suffrage, then considered the various incidental questions growing out of it, and so occupied the time until the party reached the village.

Sinclair found that the Roses, in his absence, had received an unsatisfactory but interesting letter, concerning the lost and lamented Virginia.

CHAPTER XI.

THE letter received by Mrs. Freeman during
Sinclair's visit to the pigeon roost was from
her brother, Tim Rose. It had been written on
board the boat as he descended the Mississippi, and
sent up by the captain of an ascending boat. It
contained the substance of a conversation which he
had overheard between two boatmen as he was
lying in his berth, asleep as they supposed. One
of them, a grim-looking fellow with unshaven
whiskers and moustache, turning to his companion, said, —

"Jose, what did the captain do with that blue-
eyed girl o' his?"

"How should I know," replied the other.
"Captain Leyba generally knows how to keep his
own counsel." ·

"Why, you helped to bring her to the cave, and
might have picked up something."

"Not a bit," said the man who had been addressed as Jose. "I knew the captain had a daughter at Shawneetown, long before. He had arranged to steal her off more than a year ago, but he gave that up. My opinion is, that he took her to a nunnery at New Orleans."

"How did the girl happen to be in Shawnee-town?" inquired the first speaker.

"Well, I'll tell you what I heard a year ago. The Captain told Guzman that he had a daughter in Shawneetown, which a woman was bringing up in mistake for her own; and that the woman treated the girl so kindly and loved her so dearly that he hadn't the heart to take her away."

Something more was said about the ₊girl becoming much attached to her father before the boat reached New Orleans, and the conversation was thus dropped.

It was Tim's opinion that the girl spoken of was 'Ginia Rose. He was at first much perplexed at the whole conversation between the men; but he finally came to the conclusion that either they knew he was not really asleep, or that some one of the Cave-in-Rock party had stolen the girl, and concocted the story of her being his daughter to justify the act to his companions.

"And what do you think of the matter, madam?" inquired Sinclair of Mrs. Freeman, when she had read the letter to him.

"Indeed," she replied, "I know not what to think."

"It cannot possibly be that you could have gotten possession of another child as your own?"

"Oh, no, no!" exclaimed the mother. "She was once out of my sight three months, just before she was a year old; but her father had her then, and he could not possibly be mistaken in her; and we recovered her directly from his possession." After a moment she continued, "Oh, it isn't *possible* that I can be mistaken in my child!"

"Did not this old negro woman formerly belong to Mr. Freeman?" inquired Sinclair.

"She did," replied Katy; "and the faithful creature always nursed 'Ginia while in Freeman's possession, and was much attached to the child."

"Well, there is mystery somewhere," said Sinclair. "Have you ever suspected Tabby of being privy to 'Ginia's disappearance?"

"No, I have not," replied Mrs. Freeman. "Brother Tim once thought so for a short time; but he gave the idea up. She loved 'Ginia too well herself to be guilty of such cruelty."

"At any rate," said Sinclair, "it is nearly certain—and Tim's account makes it more so— that Virginia is not in New Orleans; but with the nun Sister Naomi, at St. Genevieve. I shall visit

St. Louis immediately, for the purpose of con-
ferring with my uncle; and will then search out
my Virginia at whatever trouble. And if she
shall prove—as I trust and believe—to be also
your 'Ginia, so much the better."

At this time a line of "stations" had been
established, block-houses erected, and companies
of Rangers or mounted riflemen were constantly
scouring the country from Edwardsville, near the
Mississippi above St. Louis, to the United States
Saline Works, back of Shawneetown, and already
known to the reader, for the purpose of preventing
the incursions of Indians. Sinclair had decided
to prepare himself with a good horse, and equipped
with a rifle, to pass along the line of stations to
Edwardsville and thence to St. Louis. Accordingly, on the next morning, he proceeded to the Salt
Works as his point of departure. Here he found
Lesure, the Frenchman, ready to make the same
journey on business connected with the Salt
Works. Lesure did not recôgnize him at first,
having only seen him in his wounded condition.
When he learned that he was really the hero of
Dr. Reed's new operation in surgery, and that he
was also bound to St. Louis, he was delighted.

"Ah, ha, sare!" said Lesure. "Glad to see
you, Mistaire Seenclair. Ha, ha; first de tom-

'hawk knock in de cranium; dat not keel you. Den Doctare Reed bore beeg hole in heem with centare beet; *dat* not keel you. Ha, ha! You can go to San Louis safe."

"Yes," responded Sinclair; "I am tolerably hard to kill. I am to have the pleasure of your company on the way, am I?"

"Tank you, sare," replied the polite Frenchman; "dat weel give me ver moche plaisure."

The distance from the Salt Works to the first station was about fifteen miles; and as the small squad of Rangers, whose duty it was to pass and repass from the works to the station daily, were just ready to start, Sinclair and Lesure accompanied them.

The reader who happens to be familiar with Western history, is aware that those stations which were then common, were generally log-built "block-houses," built in such a manner as to resist the attack of Indians; with the upper portion projecting beyond the lower on all sides, to enable the defenders to fire down upon any who might approach. Those along the line which Sinclair was about to travel had been built under the direction of Governor Edwards to protect the settlements in the southwest angle of the territory between the Ohio and the Mississippi rivers; and mounted men in small numbers, and often a single scout, were kept passing and repassing between them daily.

When the party with Sinclair reached the first station it was nearly night. The station consisted of a single block-house made of logs, it was twenty feet square and two stories high, the upper story projecting about three feet over the lower one. It had been erected over a spring of fresh water; and a small stock of provisions, ammunition, and other necessary supplies, were stored away within. This description will answer for most of the stations on the lines; though some of them were real settlements, including a group of block-houses surrounded with pickets.

When the men with Sinclair arrived, they were admitted by another squad of Rangers from within, and the entrance was closed for the night.

Sinclair, not being accustomed to the saddle, found himself weary; and learning that the Rangers would start on their beat to the next station at daybreak, laid down to obtain the benefit of a night's rest. But the voluble Frenchman had been inured to midnight vigils at the Salt Works, and was not disposed to sleep so long as he could find a listener. In this he was fortunate; for a number of the Rangers, finding there was amusement in the man, gathered around and encouraged him to gratify his propensity. Lesure repeated the story of the Yankee who outwitted the Frenchman by tapping his saltwater pipe; the account of black Sol's escape with the Indian's horse and bells; and at length he very naturally came to the story of the rescue of Sinclair, and the wonderful surgical operation of Dr. Reed. Supposing Sinclair to be asleep, and willing to sacrifice strict veracity to effect, he gave the story a coloring which the facts would hardly justify.

"You will see, sare," said he to the sergeant commanding the squad, — "you will see dat what will keel one man will cure de nex' man, eh? Doctare Reed bore one auger hole in de cranium of dis gentleman, and it cure heem! Suppose he bore only ver leetle hole in *my* cranium; dere be one dead Frenchman, eh?"

"But, Lesure," said the sergeant, "did the doctor really bore an auger hole in his head?"

"Yes, sare; Doctor Reed bore one hole in de head of the gentleman, like dis monies, (holding up a Spanish dollar), and you see de gentleman is not murdared."

"No," responded the sergeant, with a look towards Sinclair; "he's not murdered, that's certain. But if he were not here to speak for him-

self I should suspect you were lying. The story
is equal to that of Jack Hays, who took a notion
that there was a worm in his head ; and nothing
would do but that the doctor must bore a hole in
his head and take it out. So the doctor cut down
on his skull and scratched the bone a little, and
then produced a grub-worm which he pretended
came out of the head."

"Is that a fact ?" inquired one of the men.

"Yes ; I know all about it."

"Well, did it cure him of his fooling ?"

"Yes ; the man went right to work, and didn't
take the notion again for two years. Then he and
his old woman had a squabble ; and she told him
he had been silly enough to let Dr. Dake fool him
with a grub-worm. ' Is that a fact, Sally ?' said he ;
' Yes, it is,' she replied ; ' I got the grub-worm for
the doctor myself !' And don't you think, the fel-
ler went to bed crazy as ever, believing he had a
worm in his head."

This grub-worm story pleased Lesure very
much ; and he already enjoyed in anticipation the
pleasure of repeating it to the people at the Salt
Works when he returned. He continued to talk
until the sentry was placed for the night, and then
reluctantly laid down with the others to rest.

Next morning Sinclair and the Frenchman

started in company with a few Rangers for the next station. And in this manner, escorted from station to station by the mounted men, they reached Edwardsville on the third day, without anything of importance occurring on the way. From thence they reached St. Louis at the close of the next day.

Sinclair immediately called upon his uncle, who received him kindly, and listened to the details of his captivity among the Indians and the succeeding events with much interest. When he came to relate his trip up the river, and alluded to his warm interest in the girl Virginia, his uncle laughed at him as a madcap, who had sported away the hours of a long voyage so pleasantly with his only companion as to permit a pretty child of thirteen to steal away his heart. Sinclair permitted his uncle to enjoy his laugh, but vowed that he would search out and find that same "pretty girl of thirteen," even though it should require years.

Receiving a supply of money, chiefly the proceeds of the sale of property brought up the river by his mother and himself in his uncle's boat, and satisfying himself that Sister Naomi and Virginia were not in St. Louis, he left in a pirogue with some Frenchmen for St. Genevieve. Finding that one of his French boatmen resided at St. Gene-

vieve, Sinclair endeavored to learn something of
Sister Naomi and her charge.

"You live at St. Genevieve, do you?" he inquired.

"Yes, sare," replied the man.

"Is there a nunnery there?"

"Maybe not nunnery," replied the man, "but
good many nun."

"Have they a school for girls?"

"De Sistare teach de girl, sometime, sare; not
moche school."

"Do you know anything of the Sisters?"

"Yes, sare; great manys."

"Did any come there recently, — two or three
months since?"

"Yes, sare: Sister Naomi from New Orlean.
You know Sister Naomi?"

"Yes, very well," replied Sinclair. "Is she still
there? Was there a young woman with her?"

"Young woman? Yes; one leetle woman, so
beeg," replied the Frenchman, showing with his
hands how tall he supposed the child to be.

"And do you think you could find her, or show
me where to find her?"

"Oh, yes; ver' quick. Wait, I show you."

Sinclair was now quite hopeful of finding the
lost Virginia; but the thought occurred to him

that any interest he might exhibit in her on his own account might seem very strange, and he could not prove himself authorized by her mother to reclaim her even if he found her; then he was sure, from her conduct in the boat, that Sister Naomi was disposed to keep her charge very closely. At length, after long reflection, he decided, if he learned where Virginia was to be found, to see her, if that were possible, merely as an acquaintance, without making known the fact that he was acquainted with her parentage, and sought her with consent of her mother. Afterwards he could act as circumstances might dictate. After reaching St. Genevieve, therefore, he took lodgings, and sent the French boatman to learn Sister Naomi's whereabouts, without letting her know of his presence in the town.

Sinclair waited all the next day; but, as the Frenchman did not come back according to promise, he began to suspect treachery, and proceeded to look for him in the village and at the boat-landing. He found the man in his boat, on the point of returning to St. Louis. On inquiring of him why he did not come back and report, he at first said he had forgotten; but, on being closely questioned, acknowledged that he had made inquiries among the Sisters, though he persisted in saying that he could hear nothing of Sister Naomi or her charge, as they had gone away, no one knew whither. The man's account was so confused and inconsistent that Sinclair did not doubt that he had been bribed to silence, and that the story of Sister Naomi's departure was false.

After remaining in the town several days in the vain hope that accident might enable him to learn something of the Sister, he went to the Religious House, which he thought must be her home and Virginia's hiding-place.

He was received by a woman who appeared to be the Superior of the sisterhood. She called him by name at once, and, politely offering him a seat, inquired when he left Shawneetown.

"I left that village a week since," he replied; "but I am certainly surprised to find that I am known to any one here."

"You have more friends than you knew of, then," said the woman.

"I was certainly not aware of having a friend, or even an acquaintance, in yourself," responded · Sinclair, somewhat mystified, and not knowing just what was best to be said.

"Perhaps not," replied the Sister; "sometimes our best friends are least known to us." Then, with a meaning smile, she continued: "I am not surprised that, having forsaken the church, your first love, you should now pursue the *ignes fatui* of two blue eyes. But I commend your good taste, nevertheless."

Sinclair, satisfied that himself and his history were equally well known, concluded that any further attempt at concealment would be useless. He therefore abruptly inquired : —

"May I ask you if the daughter of Mrs. Freeman — for you appear to know the object of my visit — is in this house ; and if I may see her, if only for a moment in your presence ? "

"I tell you truly, sir," replied the woman, "she is not here, nor even in the village."

Then, observing the look of incredulity with which he regarded her, she added : "It is so, by my faith in the Virgin ! "

"I am bound to believe you," replied Sinclair, "but no doubt you can inform me where she is. You would do me a great kindness in so doing, besides performing a righteous deed in relieving the suspense of a bereaved mother."

"To tell you the truth," replied the Sister, "I know nothing of either the person you speak of or her daughter."

Sinclair, finding further inquiry hopeless, at least so far as Virginia was concerned, then

asked where he should find his friend, the Sister
Naomi?

"Indeed I cannot tell," was the reply.

Despairing of learning anything of the object of
his search, this woman being evidently unwilling
to communicate even what she knew, Sinclair took
his leave. He spent a few days longer in St.
Genevieve in the vain endeavor to find there some
clew to the mystery, and then, disappointed himself, and reluctant to bear so discouraging a report
to the bereaved mother, he returned to St. Louis,
and thence to Shawneetown.

On his arrival at Shawneetown, Sinclair found
Tim Rose, who had returned from New Orleans
without obtaining any clew to the lost one, save
vague suspicions he had gathered from the conversation between the boatmen.

After earnest and most serious reflection, and
prolonged consultation with his friends, for the
present Sinclair determined to remain at Shawneetown, and to pursue the study of the law under the
tutorship of Calvard, who is already known to the
reader. But neither his studies nor any other
cause was to be for an hour permitted to interfere
with the search for Virginia; every faintest clew
was to be followed; every suggestion acted on that
held out the least promise of success.

As time passed without any tidings of the lost one, hope almost died with all but Sinclair. Even the loving and sorrowing mother had fallen back upon the belief that her lost darling had wandered from home and been drowned. And although this appeared to her kindred the most improbable, the mother's heart, searching for relief from the agony of suspense, rested at last upon that solution of the mystery.

Some two years after Sinclair's visit to St. Genevieve, in a conversation concerning the very mysterious disappearance of Virginia, he requested the mother to let him have the bit of paper found upon the boat by Tom Summers, which had never since been out of her possession. He took it to his office and subjected it to a most careful scrutiny.

He first satisfied himself that it was really a leaf from a small book of blank paper, probably used for memorandums, as it was written upon one side only, the other being blank. It was worn, and gave evidence of long use. He next became satisfied that it had not been torn from the book by design, but that it had been detached by the wear and tear of frequent handling. His final conclusion was that it had fallen from its attachment to the other leaves of the memorandum book, and

dropped upon the deck of the boat by accident.
All these facts (if facts they indeed were) indicated
to Sinclair that the memorandum was esteemed as
of value by its owner, and that it referred to important facts.   What were these facts?

"Angela with the black woman."

"Known only as Virginia."

"Limestone to Shawneetown."

Sinclair studied each of those mysterious lines
separately, for each was complete in itself ; and
yet the three lines were no doubt closely related.

Keeping the result of his questionings of the
memorandum to himself, he one day suddenly confronted old Tabby, whom he found alone, with this
inquiry : —

"Aunt Tabby, what do you know of the child
Angela ?"

The old negro was embarrassed, and after a little while, — Sinclair still quietly watching her and
waiting for an answer, — she echoed him : —

"The child Angely ?"

"Yes."

"Don't know nuffin 'bout any Angely," said
Tabby. But she was evidently agitated by the
question ; and Sinclair decided that she spoke
falsely, and that she could give the clew to the
mysterious memorandum. But she persisted in

her denial; and Sinclair thought best to drop the matter for the time.

Sinclair now felt sure the man who called himself Leyba, and who had dropped the memorandum, had abducted Virginia Rose; that there was some mystery about her known to Leyba, and unknown to Mrs. Freeman, and that old Tabby was in some way privy to the carrying away of the child. But here the clew was lost. Not another ray of light was thrown upon the mystery for long years succeeding.

The reader will now permit a veil of silence to cover the events of three succeeding years. They were years of bitterness to the bereaved mother, and of disappointment to the generous-hearted and constant Sinclair. All efforts to find and recover the lost Virginia had failed.

Dan Rose had returned to his home at the close of the war, Captain Summers had seen the steamboat rapidly superseding the keel-boat and the barge; and Sinclair had divided his time between the vain search for Virginia and successful efforts to master the subtleties of the law.

CHAPTER XII.

THREE YEARS LATER. — THE CLEW RECOVERED. —
LEYBA IN THE TOILS.

IN St. Louis, three years after the events last
narrated, and five years after Sinclair's visit to
St. Genevieve, occurred the trial of a man charged
with piracy. The case had created much excitement ; and curiosity took Tom Summers, who was
in the city, as it did others, to see the subject of it.
What was his astonishment to find in the prisoner
his old acquaintance of Cave-in-Rock !

Tom Summers was generous as he was brave.
He had supposed that Captain Miner had fallen a
victim to the catastrophe which overwhelmed the
inmates of the Cave ; and though he now bore the
name of Leyba, he recognized him instantly. He
sought an interview, and assured the prisoner that
he would keep his secret on the subject of Cave-
in-Rock, and would not testify against him. The
stony heart of the man was softened by this generosity. Seizing Summers by the hand he exclaimed, —

"Captain Summers, the gratitude of a man who stands charged with crime can hardly be worth your acceptance. But had the world been filled with such as you, I would not be the wretch I am to-day. As it is ——. But my *curse* is as powerless as my gratitude!"

After a few minutes of suppressed emotion he continued, —

"Some years ago I reclaimed a daughter, — pure and beautiful as the falling snow. She is the sole tie which binds me to my kind. Oh, terrible alternative! I must now disown that daughter, or stain her pure and spotless life with my own disgrace."

He sat down, almost overpowered by his emotion.

Summers now called to mind the history of Virginia Rose; her disappearance about the time that Leyba left his boat at Shawneetown, and the mysterious persons whom he had seen come from the Tippecanoe at New Orleans, and disappear in the carriage : could they have been this man and 'Ginia Rose? He ventured to question Leyba on the subject; but he courteously, though firmly, refused to make any further communications.

On his return to Shawneetown, a few days after his interview with Miner, — or Leyba, if they were the same, — Summers communicated to her kindred at that place the possible clew to the discovery of the lost Virginia.

On hearing Summers's account of his interview with the prisoner at St. Louis, now bearing the name of Leyba, it was arranged that Tim Rose and Sinclair should visit him, and endeavor to force from him an explanation of the mystery which hung about the girl whom he had claimed as his daughter. Mrs. Freeman had little faith in the success of the undertaking : she could not believe that this girl would prove to be her lost darling. But Sinclair, relying on the hints which he had gathered from the mysterious bit of paper which he had studied so long, did not doubt that, whatever might be the explanation of Leyba's claim to the girl as his daughter, she would still prove to be the lost Virginia.

When Tim Rose and Sinclair reached St. Louis, the prisoner utterly declined all communication on the subject of their search. Finding that any direct approach to the subject was impossible, Sinclair determined to try the effect of an appeal to the father's heart. He related an account of his voyage up the Mississippi. He dwelt upon the purity and loveliness of his fair companion, her confiding attachment to himself, her generous and happy disposition, and all those traits, at once childlike and womanly, which had made such a deep and lasting impression upon him; spoke of the long years that he had worn her image in his heart, and of all his vain efforts to search her out.

Leyba listened with evident emotion. When Sinclair had completed his story, he took advantage of the prisoner's awakened feelings to make a last appeal : —

"And now, sir, I appeal to your heart, — if you are a father who loves his daughter so dearly that, rather than have her share his ignominy, he denies and disowns her. Who is to love her when *you* are gone? Will that world which will detest you for your *fate*, regardless of its cause, — will such a world be likely to give either love or respect to your offspring? You deny her : who will believe you? Can you hope to shield her by such means? I offer you the evidence of five years of devotion as proof of my attachment, and you do not, you cannot, doubt my sincerity. I come to you on the verge of a death of infamy, on the very steps of the scaffold, and ask to share that infamy : can you still refuse me? Nay, more. I know the hidden springs of Virginia's heart; I know that, whatever you may say, she will not accept your disavowal, even for the good opinion of a world

which is not worthy of her. I appeal to you by
that tie which you say is all that binds you to
your kind : will you leave her to the scornful pity
of a heartless world, or will you yield her to a
love as deep and disinterested as your own ?"

"My son, you unman me," exclaimed the
prisoner.

"Rather say that I awaken the sleeping man
within you," said Sinclair.

Leyba bit his lips till they dropped blood in a
vain effort to restrain his emotion. Suddenly he
turned, and said to Sinclair, —

" How know I, — *how know you*, — that Angela,
— that my daughter has not long since forgotten
you ?"

"Let me see her but for a moment," responded
Sinclair, "and if she does not reciprocate my
affection, even to the uttermost, I will renounce
her love and pledge my honor not to reveal her
place of retreat."

"Suppose I tell you that her father's hands are
stained with blood ?" said the prisoner.

"No matter: *she* is pure as the falling snow-
flake."

"That his heart is filled with hatred to his
kind ?"

"No matter: hers has no trace of aught but
love and kindness."

"That poverty and infamy will be her only dowry."

"I know, I know," responded Sinclair. "You relent, and I accept the terms."

"You have conquered!" said the stern man. "O God, that there should be yet a man upon thy footstool could bring a tear to these eyes! My son, —ay, *my son*; you do not start to hear the title from a pirate's lips, — the adamant of my heart is broken up, — the scaffold will yet wring a groan from its victim. Yesterday I smiled at the threats of the king of horrors: he had no horror for me. But now I have a daughter and a son."

After composing himself, he took a pen and wrote the following words : —

Sister Naomi will permit the bearer to see and converse in private with Virginia.   ANTOINE DE LEYBA.

He then gave Sinclair directions to find Sister Naomi, and Sinclair departed.

CHAPTER XIII.

AN INTERVIEW. — LIGHT BREAKING IN.

WHEN Sinclair had time to reflect upon his position, he began to suspect that he had undertaken a task much more delicate and difficult than he had at first permitted himself to believe. Five years before he had been charmed by a bright-eyed girl of thirteen, into whose presence he was accidentally thrown during a journey up the Mississippi River. He had never seen her before or since, though by musing upon her image, his early attachment had ripened into most devoted love. But was not this an ideal love which he had been gradually developing in his imagination; and would the living original realize this ideal? or even so, could her heart be trusted through the five years of absence, during which she had passed from girlhood to womanhood? These very natural questions flitted across his mind as he took his way to the religious house where he was to see Sister Naomi, and, as he fondly hoped, her charge, the fair Virginia.

On being introduced to her presence, Sister Naomi recognized him, and expressed her astonishment at his wonderful escape from the savages. Without giving her time to question him as to his course since his escape, or his future purposes, he presented the note from Leyba.

"This comes from the prisoner charged with piracy, Antoine de Leyba," said Sister Naomi, as she folded up the note, with a tone of voice and expression of countenance anything but promising. " I know nothing of his daughter."

" You will be good enough to observe," remarked Sinclair, " that he does not speak of his daughter, but simply of Virginia."

" The man is beside himself! Why does he talk of a son ? Does he claim and disclaim children at will ? "

"He has lived to learn that sons and daughters may be born of the affections, — that love and charity form the true bond of union."

" Francis Sinclair," said the Sister, " do you know this man ? "

" I know that his hand is stained with blood."

" Do you know that it is the blood of your own father that stains it ?"

" Surely that cannot be."

" But it is. Will you see her now ?"

"Sister Naomi," said Sinclair, "I know nothing of the death of my father, and I must not doubt your words.   But the union of the hearts of the offspring will sanctify the feud of the parents. May I see Virginia Leyba ? "

"I know nothing of her," said the Sister.   "She is not under my care."

The door opened and Virginia herself came into the room !   Immediately approaching Sinclair in the most unaffected manner, she reached out her hand, and exclaimed, —

"I am happy to meet you, Mr. Sinclair — even in this, my day of sore tribulation."

Sinclair returned her salutation with something more than cordiality, and when he resumed his seat, Sister Naomi handed him an open letter, asking him to read it before he allowed himself to doubt her veracity.

The paper read as follows :—

The cause which prompted me to pretend that the child I placed in your care was my daughter, has passed; and I do but an act of justice — though you may appreciate it as something more — in hereby disclaiming her.   Her only relation to me is that she has been forced to receive a strange kindness from the hands of one whom the world considers incapable of such a feeling.   I cannot risk the danger of entailing infamy upon her by longer pretending to be her parent.

ANTOINE DE LEYBA.

"Sister Naomi," said Sinclair, after he had read this letter, "your words were no doubt literally true; I do not complain. But this note, — has Virginia been made acquainted with its contents?"

The Sister shook her head to intimate that she had not, at the same time reaching for the paper.

"The paper is yours," admitted Sinclair. Then turning to Virginia he said : —

"I have your father's permission, if it shall meet your approbation, to see you for a moment in private."

Virginia turned an inquiring look towards Sister Naomi.

"Not in this house," said the Sister with emphasis. "Its rules require the presence of a third party."

"Be it so," said Sinclair. "What I have to say, I am willing to say in the presence of my Creator; surely I should not hesitate to speak before one who professes to be his servant.

"Virginia, forgive me if I am compelled to pain you by speaking of your father, — if, indeed he be your father, which I now more than ever believe. I came with his consent to lay open before you an honest heart in which I have worn your image for five long years of separation and mystery. Through all that trying period, that image has grown brighter, and my affection deeper. My life has been devoted to a vain search for you. Accident at length enabled me to see and converse with your father, — for I must call him your father, though the depth of his parental love has driven him to desperation, and he disowns you."

"Oh, do not tell me that!" exclaimed the girl.

"I must tell you the truth; but his motive is worthy of a hero. I sought by all the means which a deep affection could devise to wrest from him the secret of your concealment. It was all in vain: he told me that *he never had a daughter!* At length I unbosomed all my love, — as I do now. I told him of our journey from the South; of the happy hours we passed together, and all that made that voyage dear to me. I told him of my years of constancy, and poured out my whole heart before him. He was moved, — he hesitated. I appealed to his father-heart: who would love his Virginia when he was gone; who would seek to share with her the infamy which her father dreaded chiefly for her sake? I reminded him that I was seeking you from the scaffold, not the palace, from poverty and reproach, not riches and honor; and I warned him that the world would mock at his denial: he could not disown you if he would. Nay, I told him that you would deny the words which cost so much, and share his infamy with his love."

"Oh, how I thank you for that!" exclaimed Virginia, as the hot tears coursed down her cheeks.

"A tear stole into your father's eye perforce : I had won! Suddenly appealing to me, he asked how I could know that the love which I professed would touch an answering chord in your heart. I pledged him my honor that if I found no echo there, I would renounce forever the right to see you. *Did I pledge too much?*"

The agitated girl placed her hand in his in silence. Her bosom heaved with emotion, and her form swayed from the conflict of her feeling. Presently she said in a low but firm voice : —

"My father trusted you when he had known you only for an hour ; I have known you for years."

Sister Naomi had looked upon this scene in silent amazement. At first her countenance expressed a feeling of insulted dignity that such a scene should take place in the house of a religious sisterhood, and in her presence. Then she exhibited an interested curiosity ; then an involuntary sympathy ; and at last a tear stole into the corner of her eye and nearly escaped in spite of her efforts. When the lovers turned to part, she could no longer suppress the woman within her, she rose, and reuniting their hands, exclaimed : —

"May God bless you!   May the Lord bless you! May the Holy Virgin bless you!   What God hath joined together let no man put asunder.   Surely there is some miracle here, for only angels love thus!"

Sinclair was willing to change the current of feeling, and replied : —

"I offer you gratitude, my good Sister, but I am compelled to assure you that there is at most but one angel in the case, and I fear, if measured from your standard, not a single saint."

The mind of the good Sister Naomi had undergone a complete revolution.   She had long been aware of the state of Virginia's feelings with regard to Sinclair, but had striven by all means in her power to banish her love and win her to the services of the church.   When Virginia had retired, therefore, she turned and addressed Sinclair : —

"My dear sir, I give you joy.   You have had the rare good fortune to discover and possess yourself of a wealth of love which will no doubt prove undying as it is pure.   I strive no more against it. Never have I devoted such unremitting care to the guidance of a young heart as I have for five long

years given to hers. I strove to win her to the
church and to lead her from the world, to a higher
service, but there is that within her which has
overruled it all. All have not the same gifts; every
woman may not attain the consecration of the bride
of Christ ; and it is very manifest that Virginia was
never intended for the veil. But there are other
duties in life. May the blessed Virgin watch over
her and keep her from sin in that world which she
is calculated to bless and adorn !''

Sinclair expressed his gratitude for the good
will of the Sister, and when he took his leave it
was arranged that he should be permitted to return
the following day.

CHAPTER XIV.

SINCLAIR returned to his lodgings and passed a sleepless night. He was agitated by a thousand conflicting emotions. He had seen and conversed with the object of his long-tried affection, and found that the real even surpassed the ideal. The young and beautiful being of his early attachment had developed to the perfect grace of womanhood. Her slender form had rounded into the fulness of complete beauty, and all her movements were calm and graceful. The gold of her twining tresses had taken a darker hue; and her complexion was radiant with the bloom of health. Within the deep blue of her beaming eyes, the fountains of the soul were welling up; and the clear rich tones of her now saddened voice fell on his ear like memories of a happy dream.

Then there was that constant, trusting, and confiding love which he prized more than life, — a rich recompense for any ill. He had tested it; it was his forever. And yet shadows would intrude on this bright picture; they thrust themselves darkly before his mind. The mystery still hung about Virginia's parentage; could it be that the apparently hardened man he had seen the day before was indeed her father? He had not said so, — he had even denied it; but then the very manner of his denial was confirmation. If he was not, whence his profound interest in her welfare? Was she the lost daughter of Mrs. Freeman, and this man Leyba the divorced husband? Could that be possible?

Then the acknowledgment of Leyba that his hand was stained with blood, and the assurance of Sister Naomi that it was the blood of Sinclair's father. O God, could this be possible?

Agitated with such thoughts as these Sinclair passed the night.

On the following day he repaired to the meeting with Virginia, as arranged the day before. The scruples of Sister Naomi respecting the presence of a third person seemed to have vanished; or the good Sister found it convenient to forget them. She welcomed Sinclair with great cordiality, — called her fair charge into the room, and did her best to be agreeable by striving to banish all restraint. After a few commonplace observations, she brought Virginia's guitar, and remarked to

Sinclair that he should bear witness to the pro-
ficiency of her backwoods pupil in at least one
department of her studies, at the same time
remarking that though she had found her pupil
slow to learn the lessons of the church, she could
complain of no other deficiency. Seeing that Virginia hesitated, as if the mingled sadness and happiness that filled her heart were too deep for such
expression, she gently urged her to relieve the
strain which her feelings had recently undergone by
the soothing influence of music.

"That sweet little song," said she to Virginia,—
"now you may indeed feel its sentiment."

With only a moment's hesitation, Virginia took
the instrument, and, after touching the chords to a
gentle and plaintive prelude, sang :—

> 'Tis sweet to muse over the past
>   Which brought only sighing and sorrow;
> To give our despair to the blast,
>   And smile with a hope for the morrow.
> 'Tis joyous to meet the loved one
>   From whom we had dreaded to sever;
> To feel that our parting is done,
>   That now we may love on forever!

During the interlude which followed the singing
of the first stanza, Sister Naomi took the opportunity to withdraw from the room.

"My dear Virginia," said Sinclair, after a brief silence, "where did you find those lines that so fully express what I this moment feel?"

Virginia blushed slightly, and replied,—

"Sister Naomi called it cottonwood poetry, in allusion to its backwoods origin."

"And so, my fair 'Ginia ventures into the haunts of the Muses?"

"Never but once, upon honor. These lines comprise all my poetry; and even these are the offspring of a moment's inspiration which never would return. I once attempted to recall with poetic coloring my recollection of the earthquake and its scenes of startling grandeur; but all in vain. The impressions came vividly, as they do now,—but they were not poetry."

"The earthquake, Virginia? Were you in New Orleans at the time?"

"Oh, no," said Virginia; "not in New Orleans. I was on the Mississippi, near New Madrid. I witnessed such scenes as tongue can never tell! And it was the more terrible to me because my father, who had reclaimed me a few days before, was yet almost a stranger to me, and I knew not a living soul on board. And in that dreadful night, when the earth was heaving like a stormy sea, and the river ran boiling and seething by with a sullen roar, I first learned my own strange history; and then I began to return the love of that father who, whatever may be his offences, has loved me with a fervor scarcely human."

"And thus the light breaks in," said Sinclair. "Your father found you, carried you to Cave-in Rock, and thence to New Orleans, on board the Tippecanoe?"

"Even so, my shrewd diviner. But how should you know this?"

"Oh, my maid of mystery," responded Sinclair, "I begin to untangle the web. You know the purpose for which the cavern was used, and the awful fate which befel its inmates?"

"My father told me they all perished by the earthquake. But surely you did not learn all this among the savages?"

"Oh, no," replied Sinclair, "I learned it among a kind and hospitable people whom *you* will not call savages, — at Shawneetown."

Virginia started, turned deadly pale, and looked suspiciously toward the door, as if fearful that there was treason in Sinclair's words, and that the walls and the doors were listening. Recovering herself, she said,—

"Excuse me. For five long years.I have not breathed that name; and only once have I whispered the name I loved for years·!"

"Do you know," said Sinclair tenderly, "that that whisper sank so deep into my heart that when I had forgotten my own existence I still remembered that low, confiding murmur, — 'Not Virginia Leyba, but 'Ginia Rose'!"

"And that enabled you to trace out and find my dear bereaved foster-mother?" said Virginia.

"No," said Sinclair; "you give me more credit for shrewdness than I deserve. I should just as soon have thought of going to any other town in the wide world to inquire for a lost maiden with bright blue eyes, named 'Ginia Rose."

Sinclair then related the particulars of his rescue from the Indians, his arrival at the Roses' house, and the kindness he had received there; his incoherent wanderings while laboring under the effects of a depression of the cranium,— his recovery, and the mutual explanations between himself and Mrs. Freeman; and finally his long search after the bright-eyed girl who had so bewitched him five years before.

"I fear," said Virginia, with an arch smile, "that this same long search is evidence that the doctor's newly-invented trephine did not quite accomplish its purpose. But how do you think I passed that same long — oh, very long — five years?"

"Oh, devoutly practising your *Ave Marias*, of course."

"Well," responded Virginia, "I am compelled to tell you that there was much more devotion in my prayers when the name of a certain young person whom I supposed to have perished among the savages, took the place of Mary's. The truth is, I was too early trained to the worship of God to be able to approach him through the medium of images, or the intercession of Saints."

"But how did you manage with the good Sister's lessons?"

"Oh, I first learned them very dutifully; and then I very undutifully argued their points, like a wild backwoods girl as I am."

"And did Sister Naomi permit that?"

"She could do no otherwise. She pronounced me the most studious, ready, and obedient pupil, but the most incorrigible heretic, she had ever known. She loved me dearly, and always treated me with great kindness; but she declared I was the last pupil she would receive from the arms of a heretic mother."

Then, drawing a deep sigh, she continued, —

"That poor, dear mother! — a mother indeed to me. Would to God I could soothe the suffering of her bleeding heart."

"She really is not your mother, then?" said Sinclair. "What is the clew to this strange mystery?"

Before Virginia could reply the door was opened from without, and two men entered the room unannounced. One of them was an officer of the law,—the other gave his name to Sinclair as "Mr. Thomas Freeman, of Limestone, Kentucky; and father of this young lady," he added, looking at Virginia.

"I beg your pardon, Miss," said the officer, "for thus entering without notice; but this gentleman who procured the writ and claims to be your father— Help, sir, help! the young lady has fainted "

Sinclair caught the falling form in his arms, and bore her to a sofa. Water was at hand, which Sinclair, with perfect presence of mind, dashed gently into her face; and in a few minutes she was sufficiently restored to speak. Still pale as death, she turned to Freeman, saying, "God's will be done! Do your worst, sir."

"My dearest Virginia," said Sinclair, "be calm! No harm can come to you."

"Officer, do your duty," said Freeman.

The officer then read the writ of *habeas corpus*, issued out of the United States District Court, commanding himself and the woman known as Sister Naomi, or either of them, to forthwith bring the body of Virginia Freeman, *alias* Virginia Rose, *alias* Virginia Leyba, before said court, now in session, etc. The officer, who was a gentleman in the better sense of the word, then courteously asked Virginia if she was sufficiently recovered to accompany him.

"I am ready for any fate," said she, still pale and trembling.

"I have a carriage at the door, 'Ginia," said Freeman, with obtrusive kindness. "You will ride with me."

"Never!" exclaimed she resolutely; at the same time taking Sinclair's arm, and motioning the officer to lead the way.

Virginia detested the man who now claimed her as his daughter when she really supposed it was so. She now knew otherwise; but the memory of his former unkindness to her foster-mother made her almost loathe him. When they reached the court-room, Sinclair sent a note to Sister Naomi, informing her of what had happened, and requesting her attendance forthwith.

"Who defends this case?" inquired the judge, when all the parties had arrived.

Sinclair replied, —

"May it please your honor, — I respectfully ask, as next friend to the young lady, to make a short statement of facts for the purpose of enabling the Court to decide who should defend, under the circumstances."

Counsel for Freeman objected.

The Court then asked Virginia her age and name. She replied : —

"I believe I am in my nineteenth year. My name is Virginia ——," and then after a little hesitation, she added with great emotion, "*Not* Virginia Freeman. I hope the Court will pardon me for such an answer."

"The Court is willing to respect your feelings," said the judge ; "but the least possible amount of mystery will best serve your cause. Mr. Clerk, swear this gentleman."

The oath was administered to Sinclair, and he addressed the Court as follows : —

"May it please the Court : Five years ago this young lady was placed under the guardianship of Sister Naomi, now present, to be educated and reared to womanhood under her care and protection. The man who so placed her I have every reason to believe is her father, and that her mother died while the young lady was an infant. A few days ago, with the assent of her father, and the approbation of the Sister, her guardian, the young lady and myself were affianced. If the Court so judge, I am defendant in this case."

The judge replied that the Court would hear the testimony of all the parties interested, and decide the case upon its merits.

The plaintiff's counsel had asked an attachment for a witness who had refused to attend and testify, and whose testimony was material. The Court so ordered; and in a little while the officer returned with Tim Rose. On being asked by the Court what excuse he had to offer for refusing to appear before, he respectfully replied that he would state his reasons under oath. He then consulted with Sinclair a moment, who asked the Court whether testimony as to the character of the plaintiff and his fitness to take charge of the young lady would be admitted. The judge answered that it would.

The attorney for the plaintiff desired to offer the testimony of Freeman himself. The judge said he would hear it, but added that the young lady and her father, if present, would also be heard.

To this the plaintiff's counsel sneeringly replied, "Oh, very well, we do not object."

Freeman then testified as follows : —

" In the year 1798 I was united in marriage to Catherine Rose, at Limestone, in Kentucky. A year afterwards a daughter was born to us whom we named Virginia. Afterwards unfortunate family difficulties raised a separation between myself and wife, which terminated in a divorce on her petition. Afterwards our child was sometimes in my possession and sometimes in hers. But never on any occasion was she out of my care so long that I could forget her or have the least doubt concerning her identity. At the time of our divorce my wife attempted to resume her maiden name, but never fully succeeded ; and after her removal to Illinois with her parents, some years ago, she was still known by my name. Our daughter, however, was urged — by her mother, as I believe — to disclaim the name of Freeman, and was known in Illinois only as Virginia, or more frequently 'Ginia Rose.

" Five years ago the courts of Kentucky, on a plea of divorce in my own behalf, granted me the custody of the child. I repaired to Shawneetown for the purpose of taking her to Kentucky. But her mother — or the family — had poisoned her feelings against me so that the child had learned to hate her own father ; and I returned to Kentucky without her. My child shortly afterward disap-

peared. She was sent away, as I believe, by the
mother and the mother's family, to prevent me
from reclaiming her.

" A few days since accident led me to the discovery of the place of her retreat. I saw her, and
recognized her instantly. She is not yet eighteen
years of age ; and I claim the right to exercise
some judgment in her choice of a husband."

The story of Freeman seemed to be sufficiently
conclusive ; and the many spectators who were
present on account of the peculiar interest excited
by the case, wondered what could be urged against
so plain a statement. Freeman was cross-ques-
tioned by Sinclair, who was prompted by Virginia
in a whisper on many points of which he was
ignorant.

" How often did you steal the child you speak of
from its mother ? "

" I frequently had the child with me," said Freeman.

" How long was it out of your sight at any one
time before it was two years old ? "

" Never over a month until it was a year old,
when I did not see it for about six months."

" How long was it out of the mother's sight before it was a year old ? "

" The child was with me from nine months to

twelve months old, during which time it was not seen by the mother."

"You are right. Now, do you think it possible that a mother who has not seen her child of six months of age for a quarter of a year should fail to recognize it?

"It may be possible," said the witness; "but I rely on my own memory. What has the mother's knowledge to do with the case?"

"No matter," said Sinclair. "And now, sir, suppose that after you had stolen that child of only nine months, — before a child has acquired any very distinctive features, —and had kept it out of its mother's sight for three months, the mother, in an effort to reclaim it, should get possession of another child, strongly resembling her own; might she not mistake it for her own?"

"I admit that she might."

"May it please the Court, I object to these questions," said the plaintiff's counsel. "They do do not bear on the plaintiff's testimony."

"May it please the Court, we will show presently that they do. And now, sir, if the mother should thus get possession of a child not her own, and if, six months afterward, you should steal that child away, would you be more likely than the mother to discover the mistake?"

Witness, by advice of counsel, declined answering.

"Well, sir," resumed Sinclair, "I ask you now, in the full view of the case, and on the strength of your own statement, whether you will swear that you were not mistaken, and that this young lady is your daughter?"

"I believe she is my daughter," said the witness.

"Do you swear?"

Witness did not answer, but was permitted to take his seat.

Tim Rose was sworn, and testified as follows:—

"I am unwillingly compelled to corroborate much that this man has said. Catherine Rose, his former wife, is my sister. The facts about the birth of the daughter, and her possession ultimately by father and mother, are true—as far as they go. But they are not all the truth. It was proven on the application for divorce by my sister that Freeman had been guilty of the most cruel and abominable abuse toward her,— beginning a few weeks after marriage, and increasing in enormity until the divorce. He never could have obtained an order for the possession of her child where he was known; nor could he have taken her away in any community where himself and the history of the case were known. When he came to Shawneetown for that purpose the people rose as one man, and threatened him with violence if he attempted to take the child. Shortly afterwards, however, the girl disappeared; and, as I always believed until now, by his agency."

"You know this young lady to be the daughter of the plaintiff, do you not?" asked Freeman's counsel.

"She is certainly the same my sister raised, believing her to be her daughter."

"Have you any doubt that she is the plaintiff's daughter?"

"I have not," replied Tim; but with manifest reluctance.

Question by the Court.—"Do you know whether the alleged mother of the young lady—your sister—consents to her marriage with this gentleman?"

"I know that she does," replied Tim.

Plaintiff's counsel resumed:—"Was Mr. Freeman ever accused of ill-treating his daughter?"

"I think not," replied Tim.

"Do you not know that he always treated her kindly?"

"He may have done so. I do not know."

"Is he not a respectable man, and a man of property, able to support and educate his daughter properly?"

"Well," responded Tim; "if a man who would

compel his wife to follow him through the woods when he went hunting, force her to walk after him for miles in the wilderness, and threaten to shoot her if she murmured or refused is so then he is a respectable man."

" Your name is Timothy Rose, I believe ? " said the lawyer. " Be good enough, Mr. Timothy Rose, to tell the Court how you happened to be in this town so opportunely for our cause ? "

" I came here some days since, in company with Mr. Sinclair, in search of this young lady."

" How came you to suspect she was here ? "

" We have had reason for several years to think she was somewhere in this town, and have looked for her in vain until now."

" You have not told us what led you to a knowledge of her place of concealment : what was it ? "

" Mr. Sinclair can tell you better than I," replied Tim.

" But we want your account," said the attorney.

" We had heard that she is now known by a strange name. There was a person in the town bearing the same family name ; and through him Mr. Sinclair learned where Virginia was."

" What was the name she bore, and who is this person you refer to ? "

Tim Rose declined to answer. The Court interposed, and instructed the witness to answer the question. Tim still hesitated, when Virginia rose, and exclaimed with an earnestness almost terrible,—

"Let the truth come! That person was my father, Antoine de Leyba."

The words sent a thrill through the court-room. All eyes were turned towards Virginia, and all in breathless silence awaited her next words.

"The pirate!" exclaimed Freeman's attorney.

"Ay, call him pirate, if you will! He never drew tears of blood from an innocent and injured wife; he never tortured my mother—"

The judge interposed and called upon Tim to proceed.

"Tell us, Timothy," said the attorney, with a sarcastic smile, "what you know about the circumstances which led this man Leyba to pretend to be the parent of your sister's child."

"I know nothing about it," said Tim, "and I do not believe it. But judging by my own feelings, I hardly know which would be worse: to be proven the daughter of Leyba, or to be compelled to go with that man, who is too great a coward to be a pirate."

"Witness will confine himself to a statement of facts, and omit his opinions," said the judge.

The attorney for Freeman having no more questions to ask, the witness was turned over to the other side.   Sinclair asked on cross-examination : —

" Has not your father an old negro slave named Tabby, and did not this Tabby once belong to Freeman ? "

" We have such a servant in the family," replied Tim, "and she was formerly the property of Freeman."

" Five years ago, when Virginia disappeared so strangely, did you not suspect this woman Tabby of being privy to the abduction ? "

" I certainly did," was the reply.

" Did she not have abundant opportunity, if so disposed, while living at Freeman's to change the child which was under her care, and permit Mrs. Freeman to reclaim the wrong child ? "

" If she had any motive to do it, the old hag is cunning enough," replied Tim.

" How old would your sister's child be now, if living ? "

" She was born in the year 1798, on the first day of November, I believe."

" Was it not October ?   Think a moment."

" I may be mistaken," said Tim, " I am afraid to be positive."

Tim took his seat, and Sister Naomi was called.

" Sister Naomi," said the attorney for Freeman,

with a complete change of manner, "we are pleased to see a disinterested witness on the stand. Be good enough to tell us all you know about the parentage of this young lady."

"I have known her father for fifteen years," said the Sister, — "the man known as Leyba. At least so long ago I knew that he had a daughter in Kentucky (and afterward in Illinois) in the care of a woman who believed her to be her own. The girl was left in my care five years ago, though the father had promised to bring her two years sooner. He has always paid for her support and tuition until the present time."

Question by the attorney. — "Have you any evidence that the young lady is his child, except his assertion when he brought her to you?"

"He had spoken to me of her, several years before," said the Sister.

"What was his reason for not reclaiming her sooner?"

"Regard for the feelings of the kind lady whose mistaken affection had nurtured her so kindly."

"And why did he finally take the child away?" asked the attorney.

"Solely for the sake of her soul. Her foster-mother was a kind, good lady, but a heretic."

"And do you really believe that this young lady is the daughter of the pirate Leyba?"

"I do believe she is the daughter of the man who is here known by that name," was the reply. "But his name is Antoine de —"

"Leyba!" exclaimed Virginia, in a tone which so startled the good Sister that she could not finish the sentence.

"No matter about the name," remarked the judge.

"Will you tell us, if you please," said the attorney, with much less deference in his tone, as he found the witness not likely to serve his purpose, "how a love affair ever managed to come into existence among the good and pious Sisters of your house?"

Sister Naomi related the manner of Sinclair's first meeting with Virginia, his persevering efforts to find her, and his coming to the Sisters' house with the written consent of her father to see Virginia.

When she had concluded the judge turned to the marshal, and ordered him to bring the man Leyba into court, saying, "This is a strange case, and the Court wants all the facts which can be obtained."

While the officer was gone for the prisoner, Sinclair and Virginia consulted together in a low tone; while the crowd of persons in the house was still increasing from the new interest given to the case by the order to bring de Leyba.

Tim Rose really believed Virginia to be his sister's child, and he would not see her pass into Freeman's keeping on any terms; yet his feelings revolted from the attempt to prove his sister's daughter the child of Leyba, the pirate. He used argument and persuasion to induce her to deny de Leyba's claims, trusting that the Court would commit her to her mother's care, instead of Freeman's. She was immovable.

"Come honor or shame, come life or death," she replied, "I will not disown my father. I will plead his parental love at the bar of heaven against his alleged crimes : at the bar of the world, I will not plead; it cannot destroy my consciousness of right."

Tim then turned to Sinclair, demanding if he required such a sacrifice.

"God forbid," said Sinclair. "I would resign her forever rather than see the slightest blemish fall on her life — even by inheritance."

"Oh, do not say that!" pleaded Virginia; "the thought is unworthy of you."

Amid the murmurs of the expectant audience, the officer now brought Leyba into the court-room. He was unaware of the object for which he had been brought ; and seeing his daughter in the seat of the witnesses, he exclaimed with violent emphasis, —

"Hell-hounds! Have you brought my child to testify against me? I dare you — I defy you! She will but speak of my love and tenderness ; she will tell you that the world, with all its soul-destroying laws, could not destroy one affection ; and that the shadow of a crime I did not commit, in which I have walked for twenty years, could not blight the love I bore my child."

Virginia hastened to her father's side, threw her arms about his neck and wept. When she told him the object of his being brought into court, Leyba instantly controlled himself, folded his arms on his breast, and calmly said, "I am ready."

"The witness will be sworn," said the judge. "Though already convicted of an infamous crime, the Court will hear him."

"An oath would be mockery to one who has been the victim of your laws for twenty years," said the prisoner. "The *word* of de Leyba must suffice."

Sinclair looked inquiringly at the judge ; but the Court said it knew no way to compel the witness to take the oath ; for if he were committed for contempt, it could only be to the same prison to which he was already condemned, and the examination was allowed to proceed.

"Is this young lady your daughter?" asked Sinclair.

"No," exclaimed Leyba, sternly. "I never had a daughter!"

"May it please the Court," said the attorney for Freeman, "we ask a decision in our favor on that assumption."

"The Court is not prepared to come to a decision," said the judge. "The answer of the witness contradicts the words he has already uttered. The Court will hear the lady herself."

"May the God of justice bless you!" exclaimed Virginia. "Not that I may aid in determining who is to have control of this mortal form, — God alone can control the spirit, — but that I may prove myself worthy of a father who breaks his own heart, who denies his own affection to save his child from sharing his infamy. Know, then, most righteous judge, that I elect to take the infamy with the love. When I deny my father, may I be denied by my Saviour."

Trembling with emotion, her whole countenance lighted up by the soul within, she turned to de Leyba : —

"Look upon me, father!" she cried. "Do I

look like a craven to fear the world's contempt ?
Do you read the word *ingrate* upon my forehead ?
Have I not loved you too deeply, too truly, to for-
sake you in your day of trial ?   This tongue which
you tell me syllables the very tones of that mother
I never knew, — think you it can deny you when
ignominy falls upon you, — that it can thus disgrace and dishonor her memory ?   No, my father,
I dare the world's contempt, — and will you be less
resolute ? "

De Leyba rose instantly as Virginia concluded,
and exclaimed : —

" I am ready.   Let the oath be administered, —
infamous though I be."

The conduct of Leyba toward Virginia had evidently changed the feeling of the people, and when
he rose to take the oath a sudden murmur of
applause ran through the court-room.   It was evident from the expression upon the countenance of
the multitude that they doubted whether a man
who could thus love his child, — thus voluntarily
disclaim and deny her forever for the sake of shield-
ing her reputation from the stains which soiled his
own, — could be the hardened wretch he was believed.

When Leyba had taken the oath, he began in a
tone of assumed calmness, painful to hear : —

May it please the Court : Seventeen years ago I had the misfortune to lose a dear and devoted wife by the hand of death, while descending the Ohio, just about Limestone. My child was with me. I was alone with her ; and I had not a friend in the wide world. To go down the river alone with that infant was impossible, and I placed it for a few days in the care of a negro nurse. The very next day the child was stolen away by this man here present, Mr. Rose, in mistake for another. From that day to this, I have never lost sight of her for a month at once. Five years ago I re-claimed her by the agency of the same nurse into whose care I committed her more than twelve years before. Since then she has been in the care and under the protection of Sister Naomi."

" And what became of *my* daughter ? " exclaimed Freeman.

" You must seek her at the hands of the negro nurse in whose care you left her. I can only say that had she remained in the hands of her mother, she might still be there to gladden her heart. I have done." And Leyba took his seat.

"The Court awards the keeping of the young lady to Sister Naomi, until she be twenty-one years of age," decided the judge, "unless sooner married."

A shout of approbation went up from the auditors as the judge pronounced the decision of the court.

Virginia embraced her father, who was then reconducted to his prison ; and Sinclair accompanied Virginia and the good Sister Naomi home.

CHAPTER XV.

WHEN Sinclair had returned to his quarters, he felt confused and bewildered. The depth and strength of Virginia's character, which had been disclosed to him so recently, had been a revelation to him. He knew that she was beautiful, even beyond his fondest recollections, his brightest dreams; he knew that she was generous, sympathetic, and affectionate. But he was hardly prepared for the courage she had shown, her heroic devotion to the doomed man whom she persisted in claiming as her father. What was that father's real character? What the mystery which enveloped it? Evidently, he was no common man; for with a full knowledge of his life on her part, he had won from his daughter, who never knew him until she was passing out of childhood, such love and such devotion as reflected back honor even upon the criminal himself. Was he indeed a criminal? He did not know the specific charge on which Leyba had been convicted, nor the evidence upon which that conviction had been obtained. But did he not know, at least, that Leyba was a party to the seizure of the Tippecanoe? He thought of Leyba's words, — that under the shadow of a crime which he did not commit, he had walked for years. What hidden mystery lurked behind Sister Naomi's statement, — that Leyba's hands were red with the blood of Sinclair's own father?

All these questions came crowding upon him at once; and he could find no answer. He had some recollection of hearing it said in his childhood that that his father had fallen in a duel; but duelling was not considered criminal in Cuba, where his youthful days had been passed.

Leyba had at one time — apparently by inadvertence — spoken of Virginia as "Angela;" if that were her real name, why had she not borne it since being reunited to her father. Was there further mystery connected with that name so unwittingly pronounced? He had even been led to suspect that the name Leyba bore was not his real one: was that real name stained with crime?

Unable to find rest, his thoughts confused themselves in vain attempts to solve the mysteries which for the last few days had been so rapidly gathering about him. Baffled in every attempt to unravel the tangled web, he turned his troubled thoughts from these vain questionings. He passed in review the more recent events of his life: his hospitable reception at Shawneetown; the strange fortune which had led him there in so remarkable a manner; and the clew of her lost Virginia which he had brought her mother, as he had thought her: a devoted mother, who had mourned her lost darling through all these years, and who would now find the lost one only to lose the right to call her daughter!

For the first time in his life, Sinclair became troubled about his own early history. His mother had always been reticent on the subject of his father's death, saying only that he had died while his son was but an infant. Then, while his thoughts were lingering on his new history, came to him the question which comes to every unselfish man who has won the heart of a noble woman: was he worthy of that deep and unquestioning affection which had been given him by Virginia?

Burdened by such thoughts as these, Sinclair retired to a disturbed slumber to await such further revelations as the morrow might bring.

Before leaving the court-room, Leyba had requested Sinclair and Virginia to visit him in prison on the next day, as he wished to make some communication of importance to them. They accordingly proceeded on the next morning to the prison where Leyba was confined. He received them with much emotion, taking Sinclair's hand, and pressing it in silence, while his chest heaved with the earnestness of his feelings. He pressed his daughter to his bosom and imprinted a kiss upon her cheek, while a tear traced its unwonted way down his face.

"My son," said he, "my eyes have long been a stranger to tears; and now that your faithfulness and the love of my daughter have broken up the fountain again, they burn my flesh like fire. Your hearts have not yet been seared by the world's injustice, as by a hot iron ; and the love I bear to you — the love you bear to me — prompts me to tell you the history of a soul stricken blind by the cruel glare of the world's 'justice.'

"Some of the events I am about to relate are already known to my daughter; but I repeat them to you, my son, that you may understand all ; what was my offence against the world, — and what the world's offence to me.

"I was born in the city of Havana. My father, Antoine de Ulloa——"

" What," interrupted Sinclair, "de Ulloa ? Surely you are not —— "

"Do not interrupt me," said Leyba sternly. " My father gave me a good education, and when I was old enough procured me admission into the army as a lieutenant. My knowledge of the English language, and my father's influence, procured me the situation of private secretary to the Captain-General ; and for some time I was apparently on the high road to preferment. The captain of the company to which I belonged was a man named Santa Clara. He was a proud, overbearing man — why do you tremble, my son ? Know you anything of his history ?"

" My father," interposed Virginia, " Don Santa Clara was his father. But he can bear it ; tell it all."

" My father's name certainly was Santa Clara," said Sinclair. "My own is but the English corruption of his. Sister Naomi once intimated that difficulties had existed between my father and yourself. No matter. I am prepared for all."

De Leyba continued :—

"Sister Naomi might also have informed you that Leyba is not my name. Ah, I remember when in the gay circles of Havana I was proud of the name of de Ulloa !"

"Your father crossed my path. He taunted me with the charge of meanness; he insulted me with the assertion that I had obtained my place by undermining him in the good-will of the Captain-General. I scorned the deed he charged me with, but my proud heart would not stoop to call it false. He reiterated it, still more insultingly; and in a moment of sudden passion I pronounced him a liar.

"That which I knew must happen followed. He challenged me to mortal combat. We fought beyond the city, and alone. Oh, the curse, the folly of that act! One single witness would have saved me from infamy. But there was none; we fought with none to see but God. Don Santa Clara fell, and I escaped unharmed. When I saw him lying dead before me, then, and not till then, the probable consequences of my deed occurred to me. I should be charged with murder, — the murder of my superior officer. I fled to the interior of the country. Ten days afterwards I was arrested and taken to Havana to be tried for murder, and, — O God, was it possible! — for robbery also. The body of Don Santa Clara had been found, his pockets cut open, and rifled of his watch and a large sum of money which he was known to have had when he left the city in the morning.

May God forgive the man who did that deed, and brought infamy on my head!

"On the trial I succceded in producing a challenge to myself in his handwriting. This I had never received; but it had been found among the papers which had been taken from his pockets. This paper saved my life. But I could not account for the rifling of his pockets and the loss of his money and watch; and so the law — the law which is so much extolled; which all men are called upon to revere; which is the strong barrier against all wrong, — that law pronounced me a robber! No matter that my character had always been above reproach; no matter that there was no shadow of proof of robbery against me, while I admitted the duel; no matter that such a decision would blast my hopes forever; I was convicted of theft, and doomed to the degrading punishment of the chain-gang. Oh, had it only been death! I was chained with a gang of vulgar thieves, and sent to a distant part of the island to work upon a sea-coast fortification. Here for three months I remained bearing the jeers and taunts of my fellow-prisoners, who, because I did not sink to their own low level, named me 'the gentleman robber.'

"I had not yet let go my integrity, notwithstanding this taste of the world's justice. I

endeavored to palliate the action of the court,
which condemned me, and the law which permitted the condemnation; and I fondly looked
forward to the day when, in some other land, I
should be able to stand upright as a man! I was
willing to bear exile from my native land forever,
while the hope was left me of winning an honest
reputation in another.

"One evening pirates landed on the coast, drove
the soldiers from their position, and set the pris-
oners free, offering them the protection of their
vessel. I accepted the offer, and on going on
board was immediately carried to sea.

"The name of this pirate captain I have forgotten. He was a Spaniard, and possessed the
manners and address of a gentleman. That man
heard my story through, with interest. When I
had finished he said that he would not insult me
by asking me to join his band; he wished me
better fortune in the world to which I sought to
return, and hoped that I might not have cause to
regret that I had not accepted the career as well
as the hospitality of a pirate, and promised to put
me ashore somewhere in the United States. I
learned that man's history: he too had known the
tender mercies of the unrelenting law. But to
myself.

"After some time I was put on board a vessel bound to New Orleans, and soon reached that city in safety. I assumed the name of Leyba, and sought employment as a teacher of the Spanish language. I should have mentioned that the pirate captain had furnished me with suitable clothing and a sum of money sufficient for my immediate wants.

" Before I had been in New Orleans three days, a police officer tapped me on the shoulder, and calling me Ulloa, bade me beware, as the police knew my history. My heart sank within me. I almost despaired of ever being able to get beyond the reach of that unjust sentence which had followed me thus far. Still, determined to hold fast my integrity, I privately left the city and took passage in a brig bound for New York, which city I reached after a short and prosperous voyage.

"I remained a year in the city of New York, supporting myself by giving lessons in the Spanish language. At the end of that time I could restrain my desire to hear from my father no longer. I wrote to him at Havana, still protesting my innocence of the infamous crime for which I had suffered, and giving an account of my life since my escape; and I begged that he would write to me, that I might feel that he at least had not forsaken me. I waited long for a reply to this letter. My father had never fully believed in my guilt, although apparently disposed to doubt my innocence; and I confidently hoped that after receiving my letter he could doubt no longer.

"At length I received my father's reply to that letter. Eternal God! How it crushed my wounded spirit. In that letter my own father, who had never known in all my life a dishonest thought or deed, not only asserted his belief of the charge of robbery that had been brought against me, but accused me also of piracy! I had explained the mode of my escape from the island, but he now pronounced it false, and said the police had ascertained that I had voluntarily joined the pirates in an act of piracy. Merciful God! what more could he have added to crush me down forever? And yet his cruelty went further yet. He directed his letter to Antoine de Ulloa, *alias* de Leyba; and to the care of a police officer. When I asked the officer how he found me, he replied, 'Oh, we have watched you for a year past.'"

Here Sinclair interrupted him to inquire if it might not be possible that his letter had never reached its destination, but had been intercepted, and that the reply had not been written by his father.

"No," said Ulloa. "I flew to that suspicion myself, as a relief from the thought that my father — *my father* — could have written me that letter; but I could not be deceived in the handwriting; and the conviction was forced upon me that even my father had steeled his heart against me.

"After receiving that letter I locked myself in my room for several days, meditating on my fate and deciding upon my future course. For a short time the thought of self-destruction haunted me; but I put it away forever as unworthy of me. I felt myself as wholly undeserving the world's scorn and hatred, and determined to renew my efforts to clear my life of stain. But a rising resentment against the world and its unjust laws took possession of me; and I resolved, if finally compelled to stand at bay, to defy that law which denied me its protection.

"I determined to remain in New York, where I had succeeded in gaining some repute as teacher of the Spanish language; but I also resolved that myself and the officers of the law should understand each other thoroughly. To this end I sought an introduction to the chief of police, told him my story, and asked that he would give his officers such instruction as would save me from unnecessary annoyance. I had no objection to being known to the police, and even watched by them; but I called his attention to the fact that any breath of suspicion would destroy my only hope of gaining an honest livelihood. What was his reply? Hear it, God of Justice! He told me it was his duty to *catch thieves,* and execute the laws; that the law had pronounced me a thief, and that his duty required him to warn others of the law's decision whenever he thought their safety required it. And I did not strike him down, like a dog, as he deserved! Still my visit to the police appeared to have saved me from any public exposure, although I was often aware that an officer was dogging my steps.

"One of my first pupils in New York was a young lady named Loring, — Angela Loring."

Ulloa hid his face and wept. When he resumed, turning to Virginia, he said: —

" She was the mother of my daughter, and while she lived proved to me indeed a good angel. Our attachment was mutual from the first hour of our acquaintance, and for several months we met almost daily. I succeeded in establishing a reputation as a successful teacher, and as soon as my income was large enough, I proposed marriage to Angela, intending to continue my residence in

New York. I was accepted, and the wedding-day appointed. Before the day came, a police officer called upon her father, and warned him that his daughter was about to be united to a thief. Her father called for proofs, and the law's officer convinced him that I had been found guilty by the law, — ah, the *law!* Curses on its injustice! It drove me to the contest, and I will triumph in the end.

" It was the old story, — her father was convinced and he forbade the marriage. But my heroic Angela was faithful to the end. When convinced beyond a doubt, that I had been *convicted* by the law, she still upheld my innocence, and no decision of the courts could shake her faith. But her father remained inexorable. Then she pleaded my good conduct since my escape, and urged that as evidence of repentance and reformation. What, think you, was the answer? 'Bad men never repent : a convicted thief is never after to be trusted!' It is the moral code of hell, and would forever prevent the return of the repentant to the paths of virtue. But this one frail, delicate woman turned from all else to the man whom all the world distrusted. Angela told her father that she would fulfil her promise at all hazards. And then that father, a professed follower of Him who has taught his disciples to forgive their enemies, showed how well he had learned his lesson by having me arrested and thrown into prison! We were married nevertheless. Oh, how the memory of my Angela, daring thus for me the scorn of a world comes up before me now! I see her large blue eyes, — so like yours, my daughter; I hear her soft, sweet accents of consoling hope; I recall the steady courage with which she met and defied all threats, all danger, all disgrace for me, as did my daughter, — her daughter! since worthy to be the daughter of such a mother.

"We were married in the prison; and no charge of crime committed under the laws of the United States appearing against me, I was discharged. My wife's father forbade her ever to enter his house; and she never again saw the face of her kindred. But her love made her bold, and she looked Fate in the face with defiance.

All hope of further occupation in New York was gone, and we went to Baltimore. In that city, at the end of a year, a daughter was born to us; and I called her Angela, after her mother. One saved me for years from cursing man: the other has brought me from dark despair to the consciousness of an all-directing God.

"The old charge of robbery followed me to Baltimore. Our friends forsook us one by one, until at the close of another year, we were again compelled to change our residence. Determined, if possible, to put my pursuers at fault forever, I resolved to cross the mountains and plunge into the forests of the West. Vain hope! the righteous law had not yet done its worst. We crossed the Alleghanies, and tarried a few days at Pittsburgh. Here again I was charged with being a robber; we were driven from the hotel where we were resting; and — climax of the world's sweet charity! — an attempt was made to take our child from us on the ground that we were not fit persons to have charge of it; and the law was called upon to enforce this righteous decision! But we fled the city; taking passage in the night on a boat bound down the Ohio. But the cup of sorrow was full: my Angela sunk beneath these accumulated troubles. She was attacked with a violent nervous fever on the night of our departure, and a few days afterwards yielded up her spirit."

At this point in his narrative De Ulloa became very much agitated; his breast heaved, his eyes flashed, and the rapid throbbing of his heart was audible. Seizing the water-pitcher which stood near, he emptied it with rapid and almost spasmodic swallows.

His daughter begged him not to continue his narrative, — at least for the present.

"No," said her father, "the present alone is mine : I have no future. Give me more water. my throat is burning — my brain is on fire."

More water was brought ; and after a little while he partially regained composure, and continued in low, heart-broken tones, that went to the hearts of his auditors :

"I saw her life go out. She was my hope — my solace — my saint. An over-righteous world, on the unsupported evidence of inconclusive circumstances, which would not justify even a suspicion, had branded me with guilt, and, disbelieving in repentance and reformation upon any testimony, even the most conclusive, had hunted her to the grave for presuming to bless with her love one who had fallen under the ban of its laws.

"She knew the weight of the burden that lay on my soul ; she knew how I had struggled against my fate ; and she felt that forbearance would cease when I was left alone in war against a world ; and so it did ! Can you chide me ? Even the hunted deer will at last stand at bay. I turned upon the world."

After a pause, and an effort at greater calmness, he took Virginia's hand.

"Angela, my daughter Angela, let me feel the gentle touch of your hand. Is it night already, or do my eyes grow dim?"

"My father," said Virginia, "let us come to-morrow. You are weary now — very weary."

"No," said de Ulloa; "there is no to-morrow. My tale is not ended; a little while and I have done.

"I buried my wife at Limestone, and there I left my daughter. You know the rest of *that;* the kindness of her foster mother (may the God of love reward and bless that woman !), her abduction, and all her history since. But my history since — mine ! I was myself no more. My heart of flesh was gone ; and all love left me but the yearning for my daughter. Through years of warfare with the world, that little spark of love to her who was — and is — the image of my Angela prevented me from degenerating from man to demon, and kept my hand from blood. When the world's injustice waited for my vengeance, I thought of her and stayed my hand ; when the agents of the law were in my power, I thought of her, and remembered mercy ; and when the earthquake struck my followers down, and in the midst of destruction singled out my boat and me for safety, I thought upon my daughter, and knew that for her sake God had turned away his wrath.

"My day draws near its close. The world and I are quits. When the shades of eternity close around me, I shall still live in the heart of my child, — in the hearts of my children! The world will call me pirate, but you will call me father; the world will remember my hatred, but you my love."

De Ulloa covered his face with his hands; after a brief silence, he continued:

"My daughter, I desire that you will ever revere the foster-mother who loved you so long and so dearly. Tell her your father's story, and bear her the gratitude of a dying man. No weeping, my daughter! Keep your tears for occasions of sorrow; this should be one of joy. Let the priest be brought — let the rite go on here, where I may be present. Then, when the deadly feud which procured my ruin has been healed by your union, will my destiny be accomplished."

De Ulloa persisted in sending for Sister Naomi and the priest; and the marriage of Francis Santa Clara and Angela de Ulloa took place in the prison.

When they were about to leave him, Ulloa took

the hands of his children in his, and his voice was almost cheerful as he said :—

"Farewell, my children! Your love has conquered destiny. When you come again you will not hear me murmur. Farewell!

CHAPTER XVI.

FATHER AND SON.

ON the morning after the scene related in the last chapter, and before the keeper of the prison had made his visit to the cell of Ulloa, he was waited on by an old gentleman requesting to be permitted to see "the prisoner, de Ulloa." The man who made this request might have been sixty-five years of age. His complexion was dark and apparently embrowned by residence in the South; and some slight peculiarities in his accent betrayed the fact that English was not his mother-tongue. There was a sadness in his voice while proffering his request which made the jailer observe him closely; and it was with some trace of sympathy, which the stranger's manner had awakened, that he replied,—

"Perhaps the man you wish to see is some friend of yours; but indeed, sir, there is no person of that name in the prison."

The stranger paused, in evident disappointment. Then, "pardon me, sir," he continued; "perhaps I

should have called him Leyba.   Can I see Antoine
de Leyba ?"

"Immediately," responded the jailer.   "I am
now going to his cell."

When the key had turned in the creaking lock,
and the heavy door swung open, the old man
approached the rude bed on which the prisoner
lay sleeping heavily.   For some moments he gazed
in silence on the stern, sad face.   When he spoke,
even the jailer's heart was thrilled by the anguish
of his low, broken voice.

"And *this* is Antoine de Ulloa !"

The prisoner started up at the voice, as if for a
moment forgetting that his hands were manacled
and his feet bound with chains.   His dark eyes
glittered beneath his shaggy brows, and his sunken
cheeks glowed with an angry fire.   Turning to his
visitor he exclaimed,—

"Who dares defy the world, and pronounce that
name in such a tone ?"

"Antoine," said the stranger, in a voice trembling with emotion ; "I have good tidings for you!"

"Who *are* you ?" asked the prisoner.

"I come from your father."

"Then you should smell of brimstone," replied
the prisoner, with a low maniacal laugh ; while the
vacant and restless expression of his eye indicated
that his mind wandered.

"Do you know that your father still lives, Antoine?" the stranger went on.

"No, he is dead," said de Ulloa. "The man may still live; but the father died when the son turned pirate. No, I am wrong; the son turned pirate when the father died. Do you understand?"

The last word was uttered in a loud, harsh tone which startled the stranger, and caused him to step back a few paces. Seeing this, the prisoner in a milder tone continued,—

"Look at these manacles, behold these heavy chains! Tell Don de Ulloa that the law has done its perfect work; and assure him that you yourself witnessed its tender mercies. Should he still doubt the power of the God he worships, tell him it blasted the fair fame of his son, and consumed his hopes to ashes; he will sing its praises. Tell him it left him childless, and hunted down his innocent son; he will utter hallelujahs to the Law. Tell him it pursued me for twenty years and never once loosened its fangs; he will bow down and glorify the Law!"

During this passionate address from the prisoner the stranger was deeply affected; and when it was ended asked in a tone of sadness,—

"Can you not forgive your poor old broken-hearted father? My son, look on me!"

The prisoner opened his eyes with a wild stare; and then, with a sardonic smile playing about his mouth, said,—

"So it is! Don Antoine de Ulloa, the senior! Quite a green old age — outlived your son twenty years, sir!"

"Antoine," said the old father, "for ten long years of repentant sorrow I have sought for you in vain. Your innocence has been proven beyond a doubt, and I have brought my tottering form a thousand miles to ask you to forgive me before I die."

The son was totally unmoved.

"Ask forgiveness from God," said he, "from governors, judges, and law-makers, — not their victim. Does the Law accuse you?"

"Oh, my son, forgive me, — pity me!" cried the old man, while hot tears ran down his furrowed cheeks, and his extended hand trembled with agitation.

The prisoner looked curiously at the hand which the father offered, and muttered in an undertone, as if talking to himself, —

"There's no blood upon it; and yet it joined with the relentless law to crush the innocent; it set the police bloodhounds on the stricken victim; it interposed between husband and wife, sending Angela to God, and me — ?"

He paused; firmly closed his jaws, and he looked into his father's eye as if awaiting a reply. The old man merely repeated his son's name in a supplicating tone, and still held out his trembling hand. The prisoner made no movement to accept it. His eyes became fixed, as if from muscular spasm; and he fell back upon his straw pallet in a state of partial paralysis. His limbs, his body, and even his tongue, had become motionless. A certain periodic heaving of the chest in respiration was all that indicated remaining life. After lying in this condition a few minutes a sudden throe of agony seized him, changing the expression of his eyes, and leaving him conscious, and evidently able to see and hear, but without the power of speech or voluntary motion. The old man sent the jailer for a physician, while he himself sat down by his son's bedside. He called him by the tender names of childhood, he chafed the now unresisting hands and the palsied limbs. It was all in vain. The heart still beat, and the chest heaved with a reciprocating motion; but there was no voluntary movement.

The physician came, looked at the sufferer a moment; and pronouncing the case beyond his power, retired. It was still manifest, however, from the expression of the motionless eyes, that consciousness remained. The poor old father, holding his son's hand, and looking into his staring eyes, his own dim with tears, told him how he too had suffered, —

"You lost a father," said he; "I lost a son: what could either have suffered more?"

The fixed eyeballs glared on in the silence.

"You were cut down in the hour of promise: I in the day of proudest success."

The glassy eyes wept not in sympathy.

"You were supported by the consciousness of innocence; while I was crushed by my insane belief in your guilt. Ah, how bitterly have I expiated that cruel wrong! And now that my gray hairs are ready to go down to the grave in sorrow, I have sought you out, to ask forgiveness before I die."

Still the spirit lingering on the confines of earth looked out through the rigid eyeballs, — looked, but answered not.

The jailer now approached, and in a kindly voice asked the old gentleman if it would not be well to send for the prisoner's daughter.

"His daughter!" exclaimed the old man in astonishment. "Has he a daughter?"

Before the man could answer, a throe of mortal agony convulsed the sufferer's frame. When it passed he extended his hand to his father, and murmuring " *My daughter — my son !* " expired.

Take off the manacles, break the chains from the stiffening limbs, unbar the door ! The Shadow of a Crime has lifted, and the Law's victim has escaped.

The jailer in a few brief words explained to Don de Ulloa the little he knew concerning the daughter of the dead prisoner, and told him of the wedding in the prison on the day before ; and the bereaved father went in search of Sinclair and Virginia.

It were vain to describe the feelings of the heart-stricken old man as he passed from those gloomy walls. He had been a proud and haughty man ; proud of his family, proud of his rank, proudest of all of his son — the sole hope of his house, who he confidently expected would some day shed new lustre upon the ancient name he bore. When that son was convicted of the infamous crime of rob-bing the dead — the dead his own hands had slain — all his high hopes were crushed forever. His pride hardened the father's heart, darkened his better judgment, and poisoned his life with the bitter belief in his son's guilt. And when he heard that his son had joined a band of pirates, he not only believed the charge, but strove to tear from his heart all memory of a son so base. Some years after the event which brought sorrow upon both father and son, a priest called upon him, and related the confession of a man who had suffered the death penalty. This man had confessed that it was he who had rifled the pockets of Santa Clara, thereby wholly exonerating young de Ulloa from the charge. The man had said that he had been sent to the chain-gang for another offence, and was among the number who escaped on the pirate ship. When asked by his priest whether de Ulloa had joined the pirates in any act of piracy while on board, he had solemnly declared that he had not. The father's repentance was ·bitter but unavailing, for he could find no trace of his son. As the only atonement which he could offer, he immediately obtained his son's pardon for the offence of which he had been convicted, and a royal decree declaring his innocence, and restoring him to his civil privileges. He then commenced a systematic search for the lost son ; but all his efforts enabled him to trace the fugitive only to Baltimore. Finally, after years of almost hopeless efforts, he by chance saw a notice of the arrest in St. Louis of a man called Leyba, on the charge of piracy. The description of the man, and the fact that his son had taken that name on reaching New Orleans, induced him to make the voyage from Havana to St. Louis in search of him.   The reader is acquainted with the result.

When Don de Ulloa reached the house where Sister Naomi lived, he asked for Sinclair and Virginia, made himself known to his grandchildren, and told them that for their sake his son had forgiven him, and besought them to take him into their affection.

A carriage was called ; and the old man, accompanied by Sinclair and Virginia, returned to the prison, and followed the remains of Antoine de Ulloa to their final resting-place.

Charity hopeth all things ; let it be accorded to the law's victim.

CHAPTER XVII.

A RIVER VOYAGE.

A FEW days after the death of Antoine de Ulloa the younger, Sinclair, with Virginia and her grandfather, prepared to return to Shawneetown. Tim Rose had met with Captain Summers at the landing; where he had just arrived with a boat-load of government stores which he had brought from Cincinnati; and as his boat was about to return up the Ohio with a light freight, it furnished a favorable opportunity of conveyance.

Virginia bade farewell to the good Sister Naomi, who parted from her pupil with deep and genuine sorrow, and left forever the place where she had met her life's greatest sorrow and greatest joy. Tom Summers was much gratified to welcome his passengers on board the gallant Tippecanoe, which, although a little the worse for wear, was yet tough and strong, and had just been repaired and newly painted from stem to stern.

On going on board the boat, Virginia was struck with something in its appearance which seemed

familiar; and after she had satisfied herself that
she was not mistaken, she turned to Captain Summers, saying :

"Do you know, Captain Summers, that this
same pretty craft of yours is an old acquaintance
of mine?"

Tom took the rudder between his knees, bowed
deferentially to his fair questioner and replied : —

"Maybe it may be, ma'am; but I am sure I
can't tell where or when." After a moment's reflection, he added, "yes, yes! She was called the
Louisiana then."

"But I saw her before," said Virginia. "It was
not until after the earthquake that the name was
painted over and the new one put on."

"Ah, the airthquake," said Tom. "And was
you on board through all that dreadful airthquake?"

"Indeed I was," said Virginia. "It makes me
tremble yet, even to remember it."

The pleasant morning air had brought Don de
Ulloa on deck. He had heard Virginia's remark,
and now pressed her for a description of the earthquake and its accompanying scenes; and while the
Tippecanoe made rapid progress down the Mississippi, Virginia gratified her grandfather with the
recital. The old man had already taken her to his

heart of hearts; and now hung upon her words as if listening to the voice of a superior being.

The recital of the scenes which accompanied the earthquake, and the history of Virginia's journey from Cave-in-Rock to New Orleans, naturally introduced the subject of her residence at Shawneetown, and all the strange events of her life. She talked on for so long a time that Sinclair expressed his fear that she would suffer from the effort.

"Oh, no," said she, "if it interests my grandfather I could talk for hours."

"My daughter," said the old man, "you cannot imagine what a melancholy pleasure your history gives me; and if you are not already weary, I hope you will go on. I wish to know the history of your father, — of your foster-mother, — who, you say, loved you so well; and the thousand things which you know would interest me so much."

Virginia related all the more important events in her history, not omitting her voyage up the Mississippi in company with Sinclair; and including so much of her husband's history as was necessary to a knowledge of his parentage.

"And can it be possible," said the old man, "that you are the son of that Santa Clara whose history is so closely interwoven with that of Virginia's father?"

"It is indeed true," replied Sinclair. "A strange providence has united the offspring of those men who engaged in mortal combat. May the union heal all wounds the old feud has made!"

"Amen!" responded the old man; but silence and sadness fell on the little circle. And all further allusion to the events of that fatal day was avoided.

The Tippecanoe made rapid progress on her voyage, and before sunset, came in sight of the old town of St. Genevieve.

"My dear Virginia," said Sinclair, looking over the bow of the boat toward the town, "do you know anything of that little town on the shore, with rude limestone edifices rising in the distance?"

"Indeed I do," replied Virginia. "I shall not soon forget St. Genevieve! And do you know that I was in that ancient village when (as I have since learned) you made your fruitless visit there in search of me? Nay, I was in the very house when the Sister told you she knew nothing of me! You will be surprised, but I assure you it is so."

"Why," said Sinclair, "is it possible the holy woman would tell a deliberate falsehood?"

"You asked for the daughter of Mrs. Freeman,"

said Virginia, "she told you she knew nothing of her."

"Still, it was a base and cruel equivocation. And besides, she told me Sister Naomi was not there."

"That was indeed true," replied Virginia, "she had gone to St. Louis a few days before. On her return Sister Mary told her a gentleman had been to inquire for me; and I learned about it from her. You may be sure I charged her with the falsehood. She replied that the end justified the means, — a most abominable doctrine, which Sister Naomi tried in vain to teach me afterwards."

"But even if the doctrine were true," said Sinclair, "what important end was to be gained?"

"Nothing less than the salvation of my soul," replied Virginia. "The Sister declared that my only hope was in being kept out of your sight until I forgot you. 'And how long, think you, will that be?' inquired I. 'Oh, I fear it will be a good while,' said she. This awakened my resentment, and I told her she was right, it would take long enough for me to become as old and as ugly as she was."

"And what did she say to that?" inquired Sinclair.

"She said not a word," replied Virginia, "she

only looked at me with a large, round tear standing in each eye. This was too much; it was my
turn to shed tears then. I begged her pardon
instantly."

"And are you not a Catholic, my daughter?"
asked her grandfather, who had been silently listening for some time to the conversation.

Virginia was perplexed how to answer. She
saw that he was troubled about the matter, and
feared her reply would cause him deeper anxiety.
"We Americans," she said smiling, "are too demo-
cratic to make very good Catholics." And to her
relief, the old man pursued the matter no further.

The sun was setting. It was one of those
gorgeous cloud-scenes which occur nowhere in
the world with more magnificence than in the
Mississippi Valley. The far-off ether glowed like
a sea of molten gold, where light clouds, their
glowing tints mellowed by distance, floated fair
and far as Islands of the Blest. Farther east the
undulating vapors, playing in the purple light,
gradually faded into the soft neutral tints of
mingled day and night. All nature was radiant
with the pervading light. The dark forests upon
the banks deepened to intensity of green as they
threw back the glancing rays from their thick
foliage. The very river — muddy and ever seeth-

ing in restless eddies — grew beautiful under the magic of the sunset.

Virginia called the attention of her grandfather to the scene.

"You tell me Cuba is a lovely land," said she, "and for your sake I will try to think it so; but can you rival there this glorious sunset? Forgive me, my dear grandfather. We are going with you to Cuba, but the memory of my native land will still linger with me, — the freest, the fairest, the greatest, on which the sun shines!"

"I commend your patriotism," replied de Ulloa. "We all love our native land. But this country is only a vast wilderness. Look at this muddy river! It flows a thousand miles before it reaches a civilized people. The land must remain a wilderness forever!"

Captain Tom Summers was standing near enough to hear this observation. He considered himself justly entitled to take part in any discussion on the subject of rivers; and he therefore turned to Don de Ulloa with the inquiry, —

"May I make bold to ask, sir, whether you ever saw a steamboat?"

De Ulloa was somewhat surprised at this abrupt question, but he replied, —

"I have not. May I ask you why?"

"Keep your eye on yonder black smoke which you may see away in the bend of the river. That's a steamboat. Watch her close as she runs past us."

"As we run past *her*, perhaps you mean," responded de Ulloa. "She appears to be coming against the current."

"No matter," replied Tom. "Current or no current doesn't make any odds with her. Watch her!"

De Ulloa, Sinclair, and Virginia, together with the boat's crew, now clustered on the bow of the Tippecanoe to observe the approaching steamer. A few minutes brought her alongside. On she came, smoking and puffing, dashing the foam from her round and swelling bow, much like that of a sea-going vessel, — their builders have grown wiser since,— and ploughing through the resisting current with a speed which soon carried her out of sight around a bend in the river. During the few minutes while the two boats were passing each other, no word was uttered by the party on the Tippecanoe save an occasional exclamation of surprise or admiration. When the steamer had fairly disappeared, Summers turned to Don de Ulloa, and remarked that he had now seen a steamboat, at the same time regarding him with an interrogating look, as if he would say, " Now what do you think of the future prospects of this 'wilderness?'"

" Wonderful!" exclaimed the Don, "wonderful! the problem is solved: the steamboat will settle and civilize the world."

" Them's *my* sentiments," said one of the boat's crew; and the familiar phrase will introduce an old acquaintance to the reader.

" That's jest the machine that'll do it," said Tom Summers, whose sentiments in regard to the importance of the "smoke-boat," as the reader will perceive, had undergone a marked change since his first trip to New Orleans on board of one.

" I am not superstitious," continued Tom, "nor anyway over-religious; but I jest think that Providence sent the steamboat for the express purpose of settling up this wilderness. Mayhap, you don't know how long this river really is?"

" I am told," replied de Ulloa, "that it rises more than a thousand miles above St. Louis."

" Oh, yes," replied Tom; "but that isn't the Mississippi, although it is called so. The Missouri is the real Mississippi; and that rises three or four thousand miles off, up in the Rocky Mountains."

" But why do you say that is the true Mississippi?" inquired Ulloa.

"Well, sir," was the reply, "I've seen enough of rivers to know that rivers is individuals, same as men. You would no more make a boatman who was acquainted with the Mississippi down below St. Louis believe that the Missouri was not the same river than you could make him believe he was not the same boatman in either place. You came up the Mississippi from Orleans, sir; and you saw it take in Red River, which comes a thousand miles to meet it, and the Arkansas, which comes another thousand, and the Ohio, which comes another thousand, and half-a-dozen more rivers; and you found it still the same rolling, rapid, muddy, boiling Mississippi. It didn't turn red from the waters of Red River, nor become a bit clearer after it had drank the Ohio, which is clear as crystal and almost as big as itself; and it takes in the upper river just above St. Louis, and is not a bit changed. No, sir, I tell you, rivers is individuals, and has characters of their own. You may go where the two rivers jine, above St. Louis, and you will see one of them running way off northwest to the Rocky Mountains; and it is the same muddy, whirling river that the Mississippi is here, and the true Mississippi — only they got the name wrong. But the other river, running way off North beyond the Great Lakes, is clear as crystal. You can't make no boatman believe that's the same river as this."

By the time that Summers had finished his demonstration of the individual characters of rivers it was quite dark. Don de Ulloa, therefore, expressing himself pleased with Summers' ideas, retired below with his companions for the night.

Some time afterward, when the little party were comfortably seated in the forepart of the boat, which Summers had caused to be prepared specially for their accommodation, Don de Ulloa turned to Sinclair and remarked :

"That boatman, Summers, appears to be a man of more than ordinary intelligence. Why does he not seek a higher position ? "

"If you were to ask him that question," responded Sinclair, "you would astonish him. He would think something like this, if he did not reply : 'Why, sir, I am captain and owner of the Tippecanoe, as pretty a craft as follows any cordell ; I know the river from St. Louis and Cincinnati to New Orleans in the dark ; I have been trusted with the most valuable freight for a voyage of two thousand miles without bond or witness : I owe no man anything, and want for nothing ; I vote for President, and General Jackson, who whipped the British at New Orleans, can do no more. In short, sir, I am a free and independent American citizen !' That would be about the substance of his reply ; and he would then wonder where could be found a higher position."

"Still," responded de Ulloa, "a man of his parts should be something more than a boatman."

"Not at all, sir. This very intelligence makes him the prouder of his position. In this country all men are equals under the law ; and industry, honesty and intelligence are the basis of social gradation."

"The true measure of a man in this country," interrupted Virginia, "is not so much what he is as what he can do. My mother, at Shawneetown, stands at the head of the list among the women of that goodly village, because, though she was only a backwoodsman's daughter, she could weave more linsey in a day, and do it better, than any other woman."

"There was another reason," said Sinclair, "why she headed the list ; she was believed to be the mother of one 'Ginia Rose, the fairest of the village maidens." But his words did not have the effect Sinclair intended.

The mother she had never known, on whose name her father had loved to linger, was to Virginia a sad, sweet memory, something sacred and apart ;

but she loved Mrs. Freeman with the love a child feels for the one whose arms have cradled it, whose voice has soothed it, whose care and tenderness it has never sought in vain, and she was saddened by the thought that in a few days her kind foster-mother would learn the true parentage of her whom she had so long loved and mourned, and that it would be but a little while before her departure with her grandfather to Havana would separate them forever. Sinclair saw that he had awakened some deep emotion, and said no more.

Nothing of interest occurred the next day. The Tippecanoe was making good progress, and Captain Summers told his passengers that by daylight next morning they would be at the mouth of the Ohio. When the party went on deck next morning, soon after daylight, they found the boat tied up to the shore, and saw that the water was nearly transparent.

"Ah," said Don de Ulloa to Captain Summers, "have we left the Mississippi? I was anxious to observe the confluence of the two rivers."

"Thar's the Mississippi," replied Tom. "My rudder is still in the muddy old stream. You see, sir, we reached the mouth three hours ago ; but I wanted you to see how the two rivers looked side by side. So we just tied up, and waited."

"You are very kind, Captain Summers," replied Don de Ulloa.

The party walked to the stern of the boat to obtain a better view. The Mississippi came whirling down upon the right hand, and the Ohio swept gracefully down on the left. They met, but they did not mingle. A distinct line of separation was visible as far as the eye could distinguish. Had the two bodies of water been ice instead, they could not have been more distinct; and owing to the transparent waters of the Ohio, the muddy Mississippi could be seen several feet beneath the surface, — standing up like a wall against its clearer affluent.

"This is a most surprising state of things, Captain Summers," said Don de Ulloa, after he had carefully observed the curious spectacle. "How far down the stream does it continue?"

"Well, generally some three or four miles," replied Tom, "'fore they get well mixed up."

"According to your doctrine, Captain Summers, that rivers are individuals, this may be called a wedding of the waters," said Ulloa pleasantly.

"Yes, that's true enough," said Summers thoughtfully. "When a woman marries she must either stand on the defensive, — as the Ohio does here for a little way, — or be swallowed up by yielding, and so lose her separate character, and be no longer an individual. That's just what this same pretty river does; it's all the Mississippi a few miles further down."

Tim Rose had not been well during the voyage; but feeling better he had just ventured on deck, and heard Tom Summers moralizing on the meeting of the rivers.

"I think, Tom," said he, "you must have waked up in a new place since we started. I never heard you preach afore."

"That's no preachin'," replied Tom; "it's nothin' but common sense: there's some difference between that an' preachin'."

"Where did you learn it, Tom? asked Tim, apparently braced up by the cool morning air, and disposed to quiz.

"I didn't learn it at all," replied Tom. "It is a fact as any man may see for himself, that's got half an eye. I never seed married folks get along smooth and happy where the woman held out tryin' to be an individual. It takes the husband and wife both to make one complete individual. A man without a wife is only half a man, and a woman without a husband, what does she amount to?"

"That last remark relieves *me* very much,"

observed Virginia pleasantly; "for even if my husband swallow me up, I shall at least be a woman with a husband."

"Cast off, boys!" exclaimed Captain Summers to his men.

"The wind is rising and blows dead up the stream. It's a hundred and twenty miles to Shawneetown,—a good five days' run. Good by, Mississippi! We are off."

The Tippecanoe carried a broad square sail, like a regular barge; and with the favorable wind which was blowing, made rapid way up the Ohio. The river was at a good stage for boating; and as the Tippecanoe had but a light load, and the wind continued favorable, any resort to the cordell was unnecessary. And at the close of the third day, after reaching the mouth, the boat had reached the vicinity of Cave-in-Rock, without accident or any incident of importance occurring by the way.

When Captain Summers remarked in the presence of his passengers that they would reach the cave a little after dark, and lie by till morning, because of a fog which was rising, Virginia expresses herself as much gratified at the announcement. She told Sinclair and her grandfather that she was exceedingly anxious to visit the cave, in the hope of finding there a manuscript which her

father had given into her care on the night of
their departure for New Orleans, and which she
had laid away in a cleft of the rock and forgotten.
She was aware that the earthquake had thrown
down the walls of the inner cavern, and closed up
the entrances with broken fragments of rocks
still she hoped that the spot she wished to reach,
which was at the very opening of one of the avenues, might still be accessible.

The Tippecanoe soon reached the cave, and was
made fast to await the returning daylight. Next
morning early, every one went on shore for the
purpose of examining the Cave, — the boat's crew
from the popular interest which was then generally felt in the cavern, and Summers and his
passengers, from its connection with memorable
events in their past history. When the visitors
had reached the interior of the outer cavern, one
of the boat's crew appealed to Tom to know if
that was all there was to be seen.

"No," replied Tom, "there's the hatchway overhead you see," at the same time pointing to the
circular opening overhead, which led to the inner
apartments of the cave.

"Where is the basket?" asked Virginia, as if
familiar with the place. The boatmen seemed
somewhat surprised at Virginia's apparent famil-

iarity with the noted robbers' den, and especially
with the method of reaching the upper rooms.

"Oh, that disappeared long ago," replied Tom.
"There's no way of getting up there now."

"But I must go up there, Captain Summers,"
replied Virginia.

"My daughter, it is impossible," interposed her
grandfather.

"Oh, no, grandfather," replied she, laughing.
"You may have impossibilities in Cuba, but
there are none in this country." Then turning to
Sinclair, she added, "You must help me to get up
there, *some* way."

Sinclair began to feel some uneasiness. He saw
no means for her to reach the upper cavern safely,
and yet he knew she would not easily be turned
from her determination.

"I am sure I know not how you are to get
there," he remonstrated. "Besides, the whole interior of the cavern has been demolished by the
earthquake ; and even if possible, the attempt
would be dangerous."

But Tom Summers devised a means by which
the difficulty could be overcome and the ascent
accomplished. He sent one of his men on board
for a rope and pulley. A spar was then cut from
the woods near by, and one of its ends thrust up

into the cave above, the rope and tackle having first been made fast to this end. One of the men now ascended by the rope to the upper cavern, and an empty bunk was attached to the rope below, in which Sinclair and Virginia seated themselves and prepared to ascend, the boatmen, with a cheery, "yo, heave oh!" pulling away at the rope. Don de Ulloa beheld them ascending in their rude car with mingled feelings of uneasiness and amusement, the latter prevailing as they stepped safely into the upper apartment.

Virginia took a light from the boatman and attempted to direct Sinclair in exploring the cave. But so completely had it been altered by the agency of the earthquake that she was with much difficulty enabled to recognize the ruined remains of former avenues. A feeling of sadness came over her as she thought of the fate which had overtaken its former inmates, almost deterring her from making any further attempt to recover her father's manuscripts.

Suddenly she recognized the place where she had laid the long-lost papers, but a heavy mass of rock had fallen down upon the spot. She had little doubt that could the broken rock be removed, the manuscripts would be found. At the request of Sinclair, therefore, several of the boatmen provided themselves with handspikes, and ascended to the upper cavern to attempt the removal. They succeeded in raising the heavy fragment upon its edge, when, as Virginia had anticipated, the papers were found beneath. They had been kept dry, and were in a good state of preservation.

Having secured the object of their search, Sinclair and Virginia, anxious to reach Shawneetown, hastened to return to the cave below ; and in a few minutes afterwards, the Tippecanoe was gliding over the waters of the beautiful Ohio. Before sunset her cable was made fast in front of the village where Virginia had passed her days of childhood.

CHAPTER XVIII.

IN THE SHADOW.

THE papers which Virginia had recovered, appeared to be a kind of diary in which, during a course of years her father had recorded his wanderings, and various phases of his feelings and reflections. She seated herself with Sinclair, near the bow of the boat, soon after they left Cave-in-Rock, and read the manuscript aloud to her husband. It will be given to the reader entire, — revealing the life for years of one who, though guiltless, had walked in the shadow of a crime.

And this is the city of New York! I have looked around for the indications of human love. I have sought evidence of that philanthropy which would save man from crime, rather than punish him for being criminal. Surely, said I, in the laws and in the police system of this people, who have taken Jesus for their teacher, I shall find the principle of Love. Surely they will not return evil for evil, as do those who have never been taught.

To-day I saw a crowd hurrying to the outskirts of the city. " What," said I to one of the passing multitude, — " What is there to be seen, that men, women, and children hasten thus without the city ? " " Come along ! " said he in reply. " They are going to hang a fellow ! " Verily ! Was this the Christian philanthropy of the New World?

The law of all Christian lands is based on retaliation. But the law of God is above all, and it is a law of Love. Love only can awaken love ; and punishment, retaliation, vengeance, can only arouse the very passions they seek to exterminate. Jesus taught the forgiveness of sin ; and his teachings apply to nations as to individuals.

" My business is to catch thieves," said an officer of the law. I appealed to him as a man in the name of humanity. I told him my sad story, — my conviction, my sentence, my exile, my baffled hopes at New Orleans, my flight to New York, and my subsequent efforts to gain an honest livelihood. I pleaded for justice, I prayed to be permitted to win a reputation unstained by the foul wrong that had blighted my dearest hopes. And this was his answer !

Only a few short months are passed, and I can once more feel the fangs of the law. I have loved that which is lovely ; I have sought to make Angela my wife : this is my offence.

O God of Justice, how mysterious are Thy ways ! I adore Thee, I praise Thee, I worship Thee ! When man, my fellow, fears me and persecutes me, a woman's faithful love is mine. O, my Angela, —

angel indeed to me, — for thy dear sake I curse not my race. My father, who knew my childhood, my youth, my manhood, and never knew me guilty of a a thought of dishonor, forsook me, but nothing can change thy constant love. The vindictive law followed me even to thy father's house, and thy father has cast me into prison; but even in prison thou art with me.

To-morrow we turn our backs upon the dungeon, but I have felt the world's cold charity, and go with fear and trembling: will there not be *the law* at Baltimore?

I have torn out a portion of my diary and committed it to the flames. It was false: there is no love in man. A few kind offices we had received in this city had again awakened hope in my heart. Fool that I was! Henceforth Angela is my world.

Days, and weeks, and months! and now I have a daughter. Let her be called Angela, like her mother: that is the name of love.

My sweet child! Let me gaze into thy fair face. An immortal soul looks through those blue eyes; and smiles are playing in the dimples round thy mouth, as if this were a world of joy. Sweet babe, that lookest into thy father's face with such confiding trust, — fathers have betrayed their children: dost thou know?

The law's bloodhounds pursue me still. Vindictive, insatiable Law! But we will baffle thy minions; we will cross the mountain barrier and plunge into the depths of the western forest. There, amid the wild-flowers of the prairies, and under the bright skies which have not yet looked on the law's injustice, we will rear our child. How my heart swells with the thought!

I stand upon the mountain top, I look out upon the far West. Yonder, where the sun goes down, we will build our cottage and enjoy our home. You infant city, where the hurrying waters meet, shall receive our farewell to the world.

Now, God of Justice, save me from cursing man! Do I live and breathe? Is it real, — this climax of Christian charity? My child, — they would take away my child, and give it to the care of strangers. They say, forsooth, I am a thief, and should not have the care of an innocent child. *Who, then?*

And so I am pursued beyond the mountains, and the law invoked to rob me of my child. No matter now: we are on the unchained waters of the Ohio. We float beyond reach of cruelty. This is the road to liberty. Once more I seek to live a man's free life.

Oh, what a night was last! My Angela — my wife, my joy, my hope — prostrate with burning fever, Has even death conspired against me? No, she cannot die, — though they have filled her heart with bitter sorrow ; hunted her down with the law's bloodhounds, for the crime of loving, blighted her brain with fever, and laid her upon a bed of pain, — oh, if I *thought* she could die! No, no, I have not yet cursed my race, but let Death strike away the link which still holds me to my kind. and — I am Ishmael.

Is it so, my sweet babe? Art thou alone with me in the wide world? Thank God for love: even the selfish love of our own offspring is ennobling. I see thee, my child, raising thy tiny hands and smiling on me, hear thy sweet, familiar cry, my birdling, calling for thy mother, when no mother's voice replies. Death is beside thee, and thou knowest it not.

A woman has lost her babe, — death took it; and now she is pouring out the tide of maternal love upon my own sweet darling, blindly but sweetly believing it her own.

And can such things be? Is there no hidden chord of sympathy by which the mother knows her own? Could I forget my blue-eyed child? I will trust my heart, but I will still be near thee; I will watch the tiny form expand, and see the spark of love grow brighter until thou shalt be like thy mother. I will be near thee.

At this point there appeared a break in the manuscript; after which, and apparently written some years later, was the following entry: —

And thus have passed twelve years of strife with my fellow-man. The law will call it crime; but the hunted stag which stands at bay is not a criminal. More than twelve years of strife, — and not a deed to make me tremble. But now! To tear that idol from a doting mother, who fondly thinks the child her own, — *this* makes me tremble. Alas! *thy* little one passed long since to the spirit-land. But *mine?* I must do my duty.

Virginia, having finished the reading of the papers, turned to Sinclair, a tear trembling in her eye.

"And that makes *me* tremble. Before the sun sets we shall reach my home of other days; and my fond, expectant mother — O, my dear husband, how can I deny the mother who has waited for me so long?"

CHAPTER XIX.

IT was proposed that Tim Rose should precede the others, and prepare his sister for Virginia's arrival. When he reached home, the first person he met at the door was his sister, Mrs. Freeman. He saw at a glance that something had occurred during his absence to give her sorrow. After some moments of embarrassment, during which Tim was meditating how to break the subject of 'Ginia's parentage, his sister burst into tears, and throwing her arms around his neck, exclaimed :

"Ah, brother Tim, I am so miserable! My poor 'Ginia turns out to be the daughter of the robber of Cave-in-Rock. It was he who stole her away; and the poor child is still with him, nobody knows where."

"O, no," replied Tim, astonished to find his sister aware of so much of Virginia's history. "You will see her again, Katy. She loves you as much as ever, and —"

"Indeed, brother Tim," interrupted his sister,

"it is all true. Old Tabby is dead, and she told us all about it. The old creature gave my little one so much laudanum as to kill it, and induced you to bring away another child for mine."

Tim was meditating what to reply, and made no answer. Mrs. Freeman continued :

"If they had only left me 'Ginia I could bear it ; my poor, lost 'Ginia !"

Tim felt that this was his opportunity. "Let me tell you that our little 'Ginia is a grown woman, and not a little girl," he said, "and got a husband too, — nobody but Frank Sinclair. And here they both come now, and 'Ginia's own grand-father with them," he added breathlessly.

It may well be imagined that Mrs. Freeman was startled by this announcement ; but before her surprise had time for expression, the door opened, and the long-lost Virginia was clasped in her arms.

Had this meeting been witnessed by any one who believes that there exists a mysterious sympathy between the mother and her offspring, that belief must have been much shaken ; and it is more than probable that the witness would have adopted in its stead the theory that the mother's love, like other emotions, "grows by what it feeds on." The first embrace was long and silent. Virginia was the first to speak.

"My mother, my dearer than mother, — I am your daughter still."

"Still my own dear 'Ginia," replied the foster-mother, "dearer now than ever!"

Mutual explanations followed, and mutual happiness at the glad reunion prevailed.

Mrs. Freeman related the manner in which Virginia's parentage became known to her friends at Shawneetown. When Sinclair had gone to St. Louis in search of her, suspicions began to arise in her mind as to some things connected with Virginia's abduction, when an event occurred which solved the mystery. This was the death-bed revelation of the old family slave, Tabby. She confessed her knowledge of the fact that Virginia was not the daughter of her mistress, and detailed in the most minute and consistent manner the mode by which the child came into the family. According to Tabby's account, it occurred in the following manner:

When Mrs. Freeman's daughter was about one year old, and during the separation of the parents, the father had stolen her away, and brought her to this woman Tabby, to nurse. Some three months afterwards a white man, who said his name was Leyba, came to Tabby's cabin with a child of the same age as Virginia, and very strongly resembling her. He stated that the child's mother had died the night before on the river, and offered Tabby a large sum to take care of the child for a few days, when he said he would return for her. On the night of this new arrival, the negress had given the little 'Ginia an overdose of laudanum, of which the child died. In the morning the stranger returned to see his child, and observing the woman's fear and distress at her carelessness, he proposed to her that his own child should be dressed in the clothing of the other, and the dead one buried as his own. The woman, dreading punishment, accepted the proposition, and the little 'Ginia Freeman was buried as the child of the stranger. This had happened while Freeman was temporarily absent ; and before his return his wife, by the aid of his brother Tim, had secured the stranger's child as her own. The real father of the girl, who had never for a moment thought of forsaking her, secretly watched over her welfare until he determined that the time for reclaiming her had come. This he had done by working on the fears of the negress. By threatening her with prosecution for the murder of her mistress' child and the imposition of another in its stead, he succeeded in making her decoy his daughter from her foster-mother's side, and deliver her into his hands.

As to where they went, or where they were, the negress protested her utter ignorance, and died protesting the truth of her story.

When Mrs. Freeman had concluded her account of the death of old Tabby, and her explanation concerning 'Ginia, old Mrs. Rose cut short all further conversation by calling the company into the adjoining room to supper. As they passed through the doorway between the rooms, the old lady turned to her husband and said half aside, "jest as I told you, Dan. The gal has got prettier and prettier."

Old Dan Rose was not the man to express his feelings in hyperbole, but he nevertheless replied : —

"True, old woman. A better specimen of a backwoods gal can't be found in the settlement."

The old folks had doated on their blue-eyed pet, and were delighted at her return. But the old lady remembered that when young birds are fledged and mated, they always fly away to a nest of their own. After the company was fairly seated at the table, therefore, she took occasion to say in an undertone to Virginia, as she handed her a cup of her favorite sassafras : —

"'Ginia, you won't leave us now, will you?"

Virginia appreciated the affection which prompted the inquiry, and replied : —

"Wait until I tell you after supper, grandmother, then I will leave it all to you."

But Mrs. Freeman heard both the question and reply. She immediately exclaimed : —

"Where Virginia goes I will follow, even though it be out of the United States."

"That's just what I wanted to have you say, my dear mother," replied Virginia. "Grandfather de Ulloa is going to take us to his own home in Havana."

"Katy, you don't eat anything," said old Mrs. Rose.

"I cannot eat, mother," replied Mrs. Freeman. "I am thinking of the desolation I should leave behind."

"Tut, tut, Katy," interrupted Dan Rose. "Your mother and I are getting old, and you will soon be left alone. My advice is to go with 'Ginia. I don't want to part with you, Katy; but — things are best in the long run, even if they do go agin the grain."

Don de Ulloa added his persuasion to the homely argument of Dan Rose. He told Mrs. Freeman she should be rendered as happy as wealth, good-will, and the society of Virginia could make her; and concluded by reminding her that, now the steamboats were running with such speed against the current, it would not be a great undertaking to visit her parents every year or two.

"That's sensible," said Dan Rose. "'Ginia's as much her daughter as though she had been born so, and loves her just as much."

By the time supper was ended it was agreed that Mrs. Freeman should accompany Virginia to Havana, old Dan Rose and his wife advising the measure, at the same time that their eyes filled with tears at the thought of separation, perhaps forever. On the next morning began the bustle of preparation for the journey. A steamboat was expected to pass on her way to New Orleans within a week, and it was decided to take advantage of the opportunity thus afforded to make a short passage. Old Mrs. Rose was very busy making preparation for the comfort of the young folks. She even talked of preparing eatables for the voyage.

"Why, grandmother," said Virginia, "steamboats are like the fine hotels in the city; they supply all your wants, and leave you nothing to do but enjoy yourself."

"Ah, yes, 'Ginia," said the old lady, "but they say they are terrible things to bust the biler and kill folks!"

"I hope that is rather imaginary than real, grandmother," responded Virginia. "I suppose if there was really much danger, people would stay away from them, and they would go out of use."

"I don't know about that, 'Ginia," replied the old lady. "People git used to danger, so as to kinder like it after a while."

"Well, grandmother, you know I was never in the habit of taking trouble in advance. Let us hope for the best. At any rate, while we live at all on board the steamboat, we shall live well ; so you will save all your nice things until we come to see you."

The old lady turned her face away to hide a tear. She knew it was not probable that they should meet again. "'Ginia," said she, "I never murmur at Providence, though it goes hard sometimes. Providence sent you to us, and Providence, — and that nice young man, — are going to take you away. I think it was all to be so, 'Ginia, else it wouldn't a 'bin so. Why was Sinclair's life spared, with a crack in his skull from the Indian's toma-hawk ? Why did you and he travel up the Missis-sippi in the same barge ? Why did he escape from the Indians, and come to our house to be nursed ? Why did he prove true to you for five years in spite of all the bright eyes in the territory ? And why did *he* find you when nobody else could ? Ah, Providence does great works, 'Ginia !"

"You have really made out a strong case, grand-mother," replied Virginia, "but the most striking facts extend further back than your knowledge goes. Do you know, grandmother, that I do not think there was any special Providence about it?"

At the conclusion of Virginia's remark, her grandmother laid down the clear-starched laces she had been clapping, took her iron-rimmed spectacles from her nose, and looking with an air of alarm into 'Ginia's face, said,—

"'Ginia, you haven't turned heretic with them Catholics, I hope?"

Virginia burst into a laugh. She had so often heard the religion of her mother called heresy, that now to hear the same term applied thus dif-ferently, struck her as simply ludicrous. She replied,—

"No, no, grandmother: if by heretics you mean Roman Catholics, I am still Orthodox."

The old lady restored her spectacles to their wonted position, and Virginia continued,—

"Nevertheless, I have found the true spirit of the Saviour among Catholics as well as Protestants; when love to our fellow-man is wanting, whatever our creed, we are heretics."

For want of a better reply, the old lady clapped the clear-starched laces all the faster. But Virginia desired a more definite reply, so she asked, —

"Is there any heresy in that, grandmother?"

"Elder Havens says all Catholics are heretics," responded Mrs. Rose.

"And the pope and priests say all Protestants are heretics," said 'Ginia.

"Then how are we to know anything about it?" queried the old lady.

"I judge by the fruit," replied Virginia, "if that be love, the tree is not heresy."

At this moment Tim Rose entered the room hastily, and cut short further discussion by announcing that a steamboat was in sight at the island, nine miles above the town,—and coming down with all speed. In an hour or less she would be at the landing; and all who were going must then be ready.

This sudden parting was more than the old lady could bear; so she turned to Virginia and said,—

"Don't you go, 'Ginia! I'll be bound there'll be other steamboats along in a little while; besides— besides, 'Ginia——."

"Tut, tut!" exclaimed Dan Rose, who entered from an adjoining room where he had overheard his wife's remark, "the longer you wait, the worse you will feel. Stir about and git all ready; and if we must cry a little, wait 'till we see 'em on the boat, and then it will do no harm."

All was now bustle and excitement for the next hour, trunks were strapped and baggage carried to the bank of the river to be ready for the steamboat ; friends and neighbors came to bid farewell ; and half the village gathered on the bank to see the approaching vessel and witness the departure of Don de Ulloa and his newly found family.

Within the hour the steamer came in front of the town and commenced the then somewhat difficult manœuvre of "rounding-to." She required something less than a mile of the river for that purpose, the successful accomplishment of which she announced by firing a cannon, much to the gratification of the people on shore, who nearly all belonged to a class naturally fond of the explosion of gunpowder.

Then came the hurry of departure, the farewell kiss of parents and children, the mother's silent tear, and the father's words of encouragement ; the pressure of friendly hands, and the expression of sincere regrets : then a ringing of bells, a rush of steam, and a clatter of machinery, and they were gone.

CHAPTER XX.

THE steamboat Ohio, on which the chief subjects of our story were now embarked, was
not one of those light and graceful vessels which
now meet the eye upon our Western rivers. Her
hull was built very much after the fashion of a
Dutch merchantman intended for sea service;
her bow was broad and round, her sides high, and
her draft of water some twelve or fifteen feet,
The fore part of the hull was occupied by the
boilers and engine, and the after part by the
heavier articles of freight. On the lower deck a
gangway divided the vessel amidships, aft of which
was fitted up for the use of passengers. There
were no state-rooms, as at present, but three or
four ranges of berths ran along each side of the
cabin, screened by red and yellow curtains. The
upper deck was used as steerage room for the
lighter and more bulky articles of freight. Such
was the general character of the Ohio.

When our voyagers went on board they found

the cabin occupied by various people from different places, most of whom, like themselves, were bound for New Orleans. Berths were assigned to Virginia and Mrs. Freeman near the stern window, where the ladies' department was, separated from the main cabin by folding-doors. Don de Ulloa and Sinclair took their chances among the berths near the engine.

No event of special interest occurred for several days. The weather became more pleasant as they approached the South; and all on board were enjoying the prospect of a pleasant voyage as the revolving wheels carried them rapidly down the stream.

Three or four days after the party left Shawnee-town, Don de Ulloa, in the presence of Virginia, handed a sealed paper to Sinclair, requesting him to preserve it with strict care; if he should never call for it during his life, it was to be opened after his death in the presence of witnesses. The tone and the expression of countenance which accompanied the injunction somewhat startled Virginia, and she asked with some misgiving, "Is there anything wrong, grandfather?" "I hope not, my daughter," replied the old man. "I do this as a measure of prudence. I know there is no wrong in that."

At this moment Mrs. Freeman, who was standing at the stern window, called their attention to
another steamboat which could be seen only a mile
or two behind, and which appeared to be rapidly
gaining on their own boat.   At the same moment
a shout went up from the crew on their boat : they
had also just discovered the approaching steamer.
The voice of the captain was suddenly heard,
speaking to his men.

"Fire up, boys ; fire up!   It will never do to let
the Vesta get ahead of us."

"Ay, ay, sir!" responded the men.   "Fire up
it is."

The wood was crowded into the furnace, and the
grates freed from ashes to increase the draft ; but
still the other boat was gaining.   A barrel of rosin
was brought, and the contents shovelled into the
fires.   A thick, black smoke poured out of the
smoke-stacks, and the overstrained boilers hissed
with the escaping steam.   By this time the women
had taken alarm, and sent for the captain for the
purpose of begging him to desist.   He assured
them there was no danger ; and then, as he hastily
withdrew, he closed the folding-doors which cut
off the ladies' cabin from the fore part of the
vessel.   Sinclair, Virginia, and Mrs. Freeman
watched the approaching boat from the stern win-

dows, and saw the thick, black smoke pouring from her smoke-stack, — evidence that she too felt the excitement of the race.

Don de Ulloa's heart sickened, as he thought of the possible result of the reckless contest, and he lay down in his berth to await the issue. The steam, which before had been rushing from the safety-valve with a noise almost terrific, was now prevented from escaping by tying down the valve, the captain saying it would otherwise alarm the passengers.

The captain proved to be just half right; for when his passengers no longer heard the escaping steam, a large proportion of them really imagined the danger was past. But the pale-blue steam hissed between the boilerplates, like the laboring breath of some huge monster in pain; and the whirling waters gathered in foam around the vessel's bow, in startling contrast with the sable smoke-clouds above. Over all could be heard the sound of the crackling fires, the voices of excited men, — commands, encouragements, and curses mingled in the same breath.

Suddenly there was a deep, cavernous, explosive sound; and an atmosphere of hot steam enveloped the boat, almost shutting out the light from the ladies' cabin. Some of the women, in great alarm, ran to throw open the folding-doors, but Sinclair, with perfect presence of mind, opposed them, and kept the doors closed as the only protection against the steam which filled and enveloped the boat.

Groans and cries came from the forepart of the boat. Until this moment Virginia had remained silent, but she now begged to have the doors opened, and search made for her grandfather; others who had friends in the main cabin joined in the entreaty, and Sinclair opened the doors.

Although partially cooled, the steam entered the doorway with much force. Sinclair attempted to find his way through the murky steam to the berth of Don de Ulloa, but found it impossible from the mass of ruins which lay in his way.

By this time the other boat had reached the scene of the disaster. The captain of the Vesta took the helpless vessel in tow, and himself and men did their best to pick up the drowning and aid the wounded.

The reader will not be pained by a recital of the particulars of the scenes of carnage and woe ; since that day the world has learned to know them but too well. Suffice it to say that the captain and most of the officers were among the missing, while not one of the passengers except those in the ladies' cabin at the time of the explosion escaped unharmed. The body of Don de Ulloa was found in a part of the boat which had escaped destruction, still in his berth. He had apparently died from inhaling the hot steam.

The Vesta remained at the scene of the wreck for several hours, burying the dead. Then the remaining passengers were taken on board, and she proceeded on her voyage. The body of Don de Ulloa was placed in a rude coffin, pitched within and without, and was taken on board the Vesta for transportation to New Orleans.

On the morning after the disaster, Virginia wrote a detailed account of the accident, to be ready to send by the first opportunity to Shawneetown.

She knew that accounts of the catastrophe would be carried by the first boat, and cause great anxiety to their friends there. The letter was written before Sinclair thought of opening the papers which had been left in his care by Don de Ulloa, and it bore to Shawneetown the promise that after a brief visit to Cuba, the party would return. The captain promised to put the letter on the first upward-bound boat, which he did several days before they reached New Orleans, at which port they arrived in safety.

At New Orleans Sinclair first thought of opening the papers confided to him by Don de Ulloa. It was finally decided, however, to defer this until the party should reach Havana, as the document was probably subject to the authority of the local laws.

The voyage on the Gulf was short and pleasant; and they were soon among a people who spoke an unfamiliar tongue.

After they had comfortably settled themselves at a hotel and had recovered from the fatigue of the journey, Sinclair sought a lawyer who could speak the English language, stated his case to him, and asked his advice. The man of law looked at him with a scrutinizing gaze, and instead of giving him the necessary information, asked him if his name was not really Santa Clara.

"My name is Sinclair — or was, in the United States; my father's name, however, was Santa Clara."

"And he lived here in Havana?" said the attorney. "I knew him and all about him. It was rather an unfortunate decision of the law that sent his antagonist to the chain-gang. You look just like him, and — "

But Sinclair cut him short: "I wish to prove how I came by these papers," said he. "Will you tell me how I shall proceed?"

The attorney immediately turned his attention to business. He accompanied Sinclair to the proper court, and a carriage was sent for Virginia and Mrs. Freeman.

For greater safety it was thought best to have the witnesses testify to all points which might be found to bear upon the papers. The parentage of Virginia and Sinclair, and Virginia's former connection with Mrs. Freeman, all came before the court ; then the delivery of the papers, the charge of Don de Ulloa concerning them, and his subsequent death on the steamboat, together with the fact that his body was still awaiting burial in the city.

The papers, when opened, proved to be de Ulloa's will, duly executed, witnessed, and recorded at St. Louis, in the Territory of Missouri, in Northern Louisiana ; and also a full recognition of Virginia as his granddaughter, with a brief summary of the evidence which bore upon her identity. The testator devised the whole of the estate to Virginia and Sinclair jointly, regardless of any question of identity, on condition that they should reside permanently in Cuba ; it also made provision that the body of his son should be brought from St. Louis and interred in the family vault, and the testator's body placed beside it, and their resting-place marked by the following joint inscription : —

ANTOINE DE ULLOA:

FATHER AND SON.

Separated in Life by Law : United in Death by Love.

" In the midst of Wrath remember Mercy."

The story of Sinclair and Virginia was a nine days' wonder in the city. They came into possession of the estate of de Ulloa without difficulty ; and soon, surrounded by the gay society of Havana, they began to feel that permanent residence in Cuba was by no means an unpleasant fate. Under the guidance of a teacher Virginia rapidly acquired a familiarity with the Spanish language, and Sinclair recovered his mother-tongue ; even Mrs. Freeman was compelled to admit that she had known worse people than the Cubans, — "for instance," she said pleasantly, "the Indians."

CONCLUSION.

Three years after their arrival in Cuba, our friends made a long-promised visit to Shawnee-town ; but that is no part of our story, and is only referred to now for the sake of introducing the young Antoine de Ulloa Santa Clara, who made one of the party.

Great names do not always indicate great men, and the bearer of the very long one just recited was a little fellow indeed; but in the eyes of Sinclair and Virginia at least he was worthy of his name; and to Mrs. Freeman his awkward attempts to pronounce the word "grandmother" were evidence of unusual talent.

When the little company reached Shawneetown, they learned that Dan Rose was no more; old Mrs. Rose was still alive, however, and retained her memory in full vigor; for among the very first things she said to Virginia was, "I told you the steamboat would bust her biler, didn't I?"

"Yes, grandmother, indeed you did, — unfortunately. If you had not, perhaps it might not have happened."

The old lady was shrewd enough to observe the pleasantry and laughed heartily.

Tim Rose had taken a wife, and was enjoying the honeymoon.

"What has become of my old friend, Captain Summers?" inquired Virginia of Tim.

"Would you believe it, 'Ginia?" laughed Tim. "Tom Summers is at Cincinnati, building a steamboat!"

"I am hardly surprised, Uncle Tom," replied Virginia. "Tom Summers is the man to keep up with the times."

"Yes," responded Tim, "but he is getting ahead of the times now; he says the steamboats are all built wrong, and he is going to show them what a fresh-water boat ought to be. I half believe he will do it, too."

"And I altogether believe it," replied Virginia. "It is a want of judgment to build these broad, deep hulls for river navigation."

"Why, our 'Ginia's become quite a sailor," said Tim, laughing.

"Well she might!" exclaimed old Mrs. Rose. "She's been blowed up, — she ought to know."

"And what about Mr. Wilson, and Mr. Calvard?" inquired Sinclair.

"Well," replied Tim, "Wilson has gone to heaven, I have no doubt; and Calvard has gone to Congress, I know."

"And now if I could only hear from my old friend Sister Naomi," said Virginia, "I believe *I* should be up with the times."

Nobody could tell anything about the Sister, and when the visit was over, and Sinclair and his party started on their return to Havana, they had still been unable to learn anything concerning her. The reader must trust, as Virginia did, that the Sister's good heart would still bring her friends, — however the question of heresy be decided.

THE END.

www.ingramcontent.com/pod-product-compliance
Lightning Source LLC
Chambersburg PA
CBHW021048030726
47496CB00006B/1738